CROSSED

CROSSED

CANDISE JOHNSON ; ROBERT PERALTA

Library of Congress Control Number:		2015905920
ISBN:	Hardcover	978-1-5035-6215-8
	Softcover	978-1-5035-6217-2
	eBook	978-1-5035-6216-5

Print information available on the last page.

Rev. date: 06/25/2015

To order additional copies of this book, contact:
Xlibris
1-888-795-4274
www.Xlibris.com
Orders@Xlibris.com
710454

Contents

Prologue

Morelli – Death March

March 10, 2007. Ten years since my wife disappeared and was presumed dead, or more specifically, murdered. I start what seems an endless walk to my doom in the cold hallways of San Quentin penitentiary. I can't believe my life is going to end with no closure. The walk, flanked by guards, becomes longer and longer as I near the place where I am to end my life. Where does the mind go minutes before a man dies? All I can think about is the last time I saw the love of my life and with every fiber of my being I want to go back to where she was the center of my world. As the air down the hall keeps getting colder, I smile a sickly smirk thinking how ironical it is that I am being put to death for killing the person I loved more than anything or anyone on this earth. The closer I come to the chamber doors the more I want to be told it is a nightmare that will soon end. As I hear the clang of the metal doors swing open, I know I will not wake with the morning light. I fill my lungs with air before I step forward into my last minutes of being. As the guards strap me to the hard table I am aware that for some reason this is my cross to bear. Though I in no way qualify for my biblical predecessor, I am being crucified for the sins of another and I can't stop thinking of what brought me here. Looking back and resigned to my death moments ahead I know that justice is blind and love has no soul....

CHAPTER 1

Dante - The Disappearance

I've done some really shitty things in my life, horrendous things I deserve to die for, but I would have never thought that the one good thing, the love for my wife, would have landed me on death row.

My name is Dante Morelli and I have only hours left 'till the needle ends my life.

It began Tuesday, March 18th, 1997 at 4:45 P.M. when I started to wonder why my wife hadn't come home. She was meticulous about being on time and when something held her up she always let me know, so when she didn't show, I immediately knew something was wrong. I called her office and was told that she had been in all morning but hadn't returned from lunch, which was again strange, because she had patients with appointments scheduled for the afternoon and had not let the office know she wouldn't be in. I called her cell phone for the third time in less than a half hour. Her usual message greeted me "You have reached Doctor Alyssa Morelli, I am with a patient or out of the office, please leave your name and number and I will return your call as soon as possible." Seconds became minutes and minutes became hours. I placed a call to the San Francisco Police Department and was told a person is not considered missing until after twenty-four hours. I explained my concerns. I became more and more frustrated as I explained the situation, because they acted as if I were ridiculous to be concerned when she was only a couple of hours late. They had no idea how much this was out of the norm for her. She never, and I mean never, was not where she was supposed to be, when she was supposed to be. I explained that her office told me that she had been to work that morning and had not been seen since she left for lunch. What they didn't realize was that next to me, her career was her life. She had never in her eight years as a practicing psychiatrist missed or been late by one minute.

Taken so lightly by the police, my next avenue was to call her best friend Ellen Martin to see if maybe, just maybe, she had seen her, though even her time with Ellen was scheduled. I frantically searched my cell to find Ellen's number, my heart racing. Her name showed on my contacts and I hit send. After the third ring she answered, "Hello this is Dr. Martin."

"Ellen it's Dante. Have you seen Alyssa? Please tell me you have, since no one outside of her work has seen her since this morning."

"Calm down Dante and tell me what's going on," she replied sounding a bit worried herself. She knew, as well as I, that Alyssa was supposed to be home and if she wasn't something was amiss.

"I came home this afternoon and saw that Alyssa had not been home from work. So, I called her office and they said she had reported to work in the AM and had not been seen since she left for lunch. You know this is not like her."

"Oh God Dante!"

"What? Fuck, Ellen don't do this! What?"

"I was supposed to have lunch with her this afternoon, but she cancelled. I just figured she was working through since she didn't say why. Have you tried her cell phone? Have you called the police? Called hospitals?"

"Cell's off. I called the police and they gave me that bullshit about having to be missing at least twenty-four hours. They thought I was a damn idiot for worrying already. Can you please call around her circle of friends? You know them better than I do. I have some friends in the San Francisco Police Department I'll see if they can pull some strings for me".

"I'll start calling around and be right over. I'll call Dave to see if he knows anyone in the police station that can help."

"Thanks Ellen, see you soon."

"Oh God please let her be ok" I thought, though something told me she wasn't.

I called friends in the department to see if they could lend a hand. And knowing what I know now, I think it might have been my downfall. I started with my friend Brian Deecon in the Narcotics Division. He knew us well enough to know my concerns were valid. He said he would get someone on it right away and he would stop by when he got off.

Brian and I grew up in San Francisco and were childhood friends. We stayed friends, even though we were on the opposite end of the spectrum as far as the law was concerned. He knew my love for Alyssa was genuine. He was around during our courting days and would always remind me of how dumb I acted when she was around.

I paced around the house waiting for the phone to ring or the door to open, hoping against hope for the smallest sign that I was being an idiot. However, my instincts were sharp, always had been, that's why I was good at my job. I couldn't help but think the worst. I have enemies, lots of them and I was truly frightened for my wife's safety.

My thoughts were interrupted by the doorbell ringing. It took me a minute to break my reverie and the person on the other side of the door impatiently hit the bell incessantly.

"I'm coming" I yelled.

"It's me, Ellen." she yelled back.

"Hi Ellen, please tell me you have heard something, anything." I knew I was begging. I was desperate and I didn't care. Next to my wife Ellen was the second most beautiful woman I know. She came through the door in a flurry. Her auburn hair was coming out of a bun at the back of her head as she nervously moved a strand out of her face. Her blue eyes looked worried. She looked me eye to eye since she stood nearly six feet, which looked good on her thin frame.

"I tried everyone and no one has seen her. Any luck with the police? She asked."

"I have a friend working on it right now and he called on some friends to help out."

Ellen's phone began to ring. We both looked at each other hopefully as she searched her handbag for her cell. She looked at the screen. "It's Dave maybe he has some good news" she said as she pushed a button and put him on speaker.

"Hi Babe. Got your message, what the hell is going on?" Dave asked.

"Alyssa hasn't come home and no one has heard from her since before noon when she left the office."

"Ellen, I saw her this afternoon. She came to see me about a malpractice suit she has coming up. She left around 1:00 P.M. and said she was heading back to the office."

"Dante is going nuts here. We've called everyone that knows her, the police and all the hospitals. I'm over here now, and we could use your help, so please hurry, but drive careful. Love you."

"On my way."

"What the fuck was Alyssa doing with Dave? She had no malpractice suits pending or she would have said something to me."

"Stop yelling Dante you're scaring me. You know as much as I do. Why are you acting this way?"

"Sorry Ellen, I know I sound crazy, but you have to understand my frustration right now." I was not getting the answers I needed and I was scared.

"I understand, but we have to stay calm, so we can figure out what happened to Alyssa. Going off the deep end isn't going to help anyone right now."

I started to say "I know," when the doorbell rang again.

I couldn't even muster the energy to go to the door, "Who is it?"

"It's Brian, I'm coming in D!" I felt good just seeing Brian. He still had that boyish look about him with his curly blonde hair and big blue eyes. He was my opposite. He would draw women in with his surfer boy charm, but they would fall for my dark, brooding Italian lover appearance. I used to constantly tease him that I always got the girl.

After he opened the door he came across the living room to shake my hand and embrace as we always had. "How are you pal? I can't imagine what you are going through right now. I had missing persons put an all points bulletin out as soon as you called. I have another detective from the missing person's unit on his way. So don't worry D we will do everything possible to find her."

"Thanks. B. you remember Ellen." I said as my ingrained manners kicked in.

"Hi Ellen, how are you?" he said as he reached over and gave her a hug.

"As well as can be expected Brian" she replied.

"Let's start from the beginning, tell me everything and I mean everything if you really want my help" Brian said.

"Well you know what I told you B. this evening when I called." again the doorbell proved an interruption

"That must be Mike, he has worked missing persons and homicides. He's the best."

"Homicides?" I asked my heart stopping and my body freezing.

"Relax Dante. I just want you to know whatever this man does he does well." Brian soothed. I'll get the door." He again repeated "relax". Then he yelled "Hang on" as he made his way to the door. As he opened the door I heard him say, 'Hi Mike thanks for doing me this favor, come on in." My body still stiff with panic Brian softly said "Hey D. this is Lt. Mike Senetti. If anybody can help us get Alyssa home safe it will be him." I nodded at him, not trusting myself to speak. It all seemed overwhelming as it hit me that my wife really was missing and the word homicide echoed through my thoughts.

Lt. Mike Senetti looked around and Ellen jumped forward, "Hello Mr. Senetti, Dr. Ellen Martin. I'm glad you're here."

Lt. Senetti shook her hand then suggested we all sit down and let him get some information. He wasted no time, "Let's start with you Mr. Morelli, give me her full name, date of birth, height, weight, hair and eye color. What was your wife wearing? Do you have any current pictures? When was the time you last saw her? What type of car does she drive? When was the last time she was seen? Understand that there is no detail that is too small so please tell me anything that you can."

"Her full name is Alyssa Fay Morelli; she was born July 22, 1959 and is 39 years old; she has light brown hair and hazel eyes; she weighs around 135 and is 5 foot 8 inches. She always dresses professionally and was wearing a blue pinstriped suit dress. And the last time I saw her was this morning when she left for work. She was driving a 1997 Mercedes SL500."

"Ok, now I am going to ask questions that might upset you, but again I have to ask. For the sake of Alyssa I need you to be honest about everything. Let's start with your day, tell me what happened from the time you both woke up this morning."

I hesitated, collecting myself, then began, "Well we woke like any other morning, made breakfast and left for work. My office is in North Beach and she has her office in the Sunset District near the University of California Medical Center, San Francisco. I kissed her goodbye, like I always do, and told her that I loved her. She left around 7:30 A.M. to start at 8:00 A.M. since her office is only a fifteen minute drive from here." In my mind I saw her driving away as she held up two crossed fingers. I crossed my middle finger over the top of my pointer finger. That was our sign. It meant 'I love you.' It didn't matter where we were, in a crowd of people, or just starting our day, that sign was our signal to each other. My heart ached as I remembered, but I didn't mention it as I continued. "Nothing out of the ordinary as far as the morning goes. I got home around 4:45 P.M. and noticed she had not been home yet. She is usually home before me and getting things started for dinner. She runs a tight schedule. Not only does she have a demanding job, but she has so many other projects that she works on, like her charities and hospitals where she volunteers, but we always made time for us to be together for dinner, always. So, when she was late, which she never is, I called her office to hear that she was there in the morning, left for lunch, and never returned. What made it odd was she had scheduled afternoon patients and she didn't call her secretary with an explanation. For Alyssa to miss work it has to be a near catastrophe and if she does, she is the kind of person who would call the office with detailed instructions. She would never, not call. That's when I phoned the police and was told about this stupid twenty-four hour rule."

As I looked at Senetti I could feel him looking at me as if I were full of shit. I admit I'm no choirboy, and the cops have never been my best friends, with the exception of B., but my love for Alyssa made me keep control, though I felt like slapping his smug face.

"What was the last thing she said to you before she left?"

"I just told you 'I love you'" and again I thought of her crossed fingers.

Senetti glanced at his notes "No you didn't, you said you told her 'I love you' but never said she replied. Is it possible you had an argument the night before and she left today to cool off or to get a rise from you? I'm just asking Mr. Morelli, it happens all the time."

I felt like exploding "Are you kidding me with this shit? My wife is missing and you are asking me if she said she loved me or not or if we had a disagreement? Are you fuckin' kidding me with this shit?"

I looked directly in his eyes "My wife is missing and I really don't have the time for this. Yes she said she loved me and no we didn't have some fucking argument. So, Mr. Senetti, I would really appreciate it if you'd quit wasting my fucking time and find out why my wife is missing or get the hell out of my house."

Senetti didn't seem in the least shook by my outburst "I explained to you that some of these questions might be negative in nature, but they are procedure, and they are necessary. I have to know everything that happened in the last couple of days and just for your information, my only concern here is the safe return of you wife, so none of your ranting and raving is going to deter me from my end result. So please, Mr. Morelli, relax."

I gritted my teeth, "Well then let's get down to questions that pertain to her missing and not start from step one in 'gee I want to be a detective class'. You have to understand, this is frustrating and I just want my wife home."

Brian put his hand on my shoulder and whispered, "D, he's only here to help out. The more we all cooperate, the faster we can get to the bottom of this and figure out where Alyssa might have gone."

I sighed resignedly. I'll do whatever I have to do, but wasting precious minutes wasn't one of them. I hurriedly asked "So what else do you need? I've given you all I know from this morning, except, that the last person that I know that saw her was Ellen's husband, Dave Martin. Dave had an appointment with her at noon in regards to a malpractice suit, so from my understanding, he was the last to see her since she didn't return to work."

Ellen cut in sharply, "Dante, I resent you making it sound like Dave was the last to see her. We don't know that."

Senetti turned to Ellen "Dr. Martin, when was the last time you spoke with your husband?"

"I spoke with him right after Dante called me. That's when he told me he had an appointment with her at noon to discuss a malpractice suit. He said she left there shortly after 1:00 since he had another appointment. He should be here shortly."

Senetti looked at me and asked "Mr. Morelli, did you know that she had an appointment with Mr. Martin or that she had a malpractice suit?"

"No, I didn't, but then again I don't typically keep track of her daily appointments; however, I also didn't know she was having any malpractice issues," I admitted. That seemed strange to me, since Alyssa never hid anything from me.

Senetti came back with "So is it safe to say, communication between you was not that strong?"

I stood up and looked Senetti right in the eyes and slapped his notepad out of his hands "Get the fuck out of my house. How dare you undermine my relationship with my wife."

Brian quickly stood and placed himself between Senetti and me "Look at me, D, look at me. I know how you feel about Alyssa, so I'm here with you and I know what you're going through must be awful, but you have to do this."

As I was trying to collect myself, I was again interrupted by the god forsaken doorbell. "COME IN!" I yelled. It was Dave Martin, Ellen's, husband. Dave is nice enough looking, with a full head of dark brown hair. He has a slight build and puts up a good front, but is a pushover if someone stands up to him.

"I came as soon as I could. Hi my name is Dave Martin, attorney at law, I represent Dante Morelli" he said as he looked at Lt. Senetti and Brian and put out his hand gripping theirs in a strong shake. "So where are we?"

Senetti said "I'm sorry did I miss something? Why would you be representing Dante Morelli?"

"I'm sorry Mr. Senetti, you misunderstood, I represent Mr. Morelli in all legal and business matters. And I am also a family friend. Alyssa and my wife are friends from medical school. So, if you don't mind, can you please bring me up to speed?"

Senetti looked at Dave with contempt as if he were just another obstacle in finding me guilty of my wife's disappearance. "I don't believe I need to bring you up to speed as you say. We don't even know if there is a missing person yet. I am merely trying to get information, so I can put out a bulletin. But I would like to know what Mrs. Morelli was doing at your office, since it seems you were the last to see her this afternoon."

Dave began "Alyssa called me early this morning to discuss a client that had threatened her with malpractice. She had appointments all morning, as did I, so I scheduled an appointment at noon over lunch.

She showed up at my office, prompt as always and we discussed the issue at hand, which was the malpractice suit. She didn't want to go into too much detail due to patient confidentiality, but wanted some legal advice. We discussed it for about an hour and she left. She seemed upset, but in control. I was as shocked as anyone when my wife told me that she hadn't come home."

"What did you do after she left?" Senetti inquired.

"I prepared for my next appointment, since I was already late for my one o'clock. That appointment lasted about three hours. You can call my office and verify my appointment and time with my client with my assistant Cathy Moore."

Senetti replied, "I am going to place a couple of calls and get this moving. I will need to look around the house and the property Mr.Morelli. I hope you don't mind?"

"Yes I do mind, but if it will speed things up go ahead. The only place I can't allow you to go into is my office."

Senetti nodded consent, but I could see there were going to be problems between the two of us.

CHAPTER 2

Senetti – The Investigation

$\mathcal{I}$ nodded my consent, but I thought "We'll see about that. Wonder what is in his office."

"I won't be long, but I would like to start in the master bedroom. Can you show me the way?"

"I'll show you around." Dr. Ellen Martin said. "Dante can stay here."

Again I nodded consent. I was thankful I could have a few minutes break from Morelli he was a time bomb. And I have to admit Dr. Martin's backside afforded a much better view as I followed her up the stairs to the bedroom. Ascending to the second level it became apparent that Mr. Morelli and his wife seemed to enjoy life and each other. I could see picture upon picture on almost every wall of them together: on a beach in bathing suits, wearing khakis on an African Safari, the trendy clothes of Paris with the Eiffel Tower in the background. Everywhere I looked their smiling faces stared back at me.

The house was enormous and walking down the hallway to the master bedroom I noticed how organized and immaculate everything was. The bedroom was the same. It almost seemed sterile it was so white and so clean. I asked Dr. Martin if the Morelli's had a maid or a service to clean their house.

She replied "No I don't think so, since Alyssa likes cleaning her own house. She has never felt like anyone can do it as well as she can. She never wanted anyone else looking at or cleaning her things. She is a perfectionist and actually a little anal when it comes to her house."

It didn't come as a surprise to me. Alyssa Morelli was never late, never missed work, and never left a thing out of place in her home or in her life it seemed. I had a feeling I wasn't going to find a thing in this bedroom or this house, but just the same I called the Crime Scene Unit to come and do a clean sweep of the house. Morelli wouldn't like it, but if he wanted his wife back he would do what I wanted and I had a gut feeling someone in my present company wasn't telling me everything.

I put in a call to the unit and as soon as I got an answer I said, "This is Lt. Senetti. I need CSI to do a sweep on the Morelli House for a missing person's case and I need it yesterday if you know what I mean."

"Affirmative. Lieutenant."

"The address is 3244 Langer Ave. in the North Beach district, copy that."

"Affirmative Lt. will dispatch and confirm."

This decided, I descended the stairs and broke the news. "Ok folks we are going to have CSI do a sweep of the house so I need everyone to cooperate. As a precaution I would like everyone to step outside while we conduct the investigation, that means everyone, no exceptions", I said as I glared at Morelli, noticing him shaking his head.

Morelli looked at me quizzically "Do you seriously think you will find anything here?"

I apologized, "Mr. Morelli I'm sorry to have to do this in your home, but at this time we have no idea where your wife is and we need to start somewhere."

Brian had been sitting quietly, but at this he pulled me aside "What the hell is going on Mike?" He asked heatedly.

"I am doing what you asked me to do Brian; investigating the disappearance of Dr. Alyssa Morelli, what the hell does it look like."

"So why CSI? We don't even know if she is missing yet. She could have gone for a long walk for all we know. Your pulling out red flags a little early don't you think."

"From the little time I have been here I think it is warranted. She hasn't been seen since early this afternoon; she never misses an appointment; she always has dinner on time with her husband. This woman seems to be one of the most predictable females I have ever encountered. It just doesn't add up. There may be absolutely nothing here, but we are going on over seven hours since she was last seen. I believe there is no time to waste here Brian. Let me do my fucking job!"

"You know who Morelli is, the press is going to have field day with this if they get wind that she is missing." Brian countered.

This pissed me off "Who are you most concerned about Alyssa being found or protecting your buddy?"

"Fuck you Mike, don't even imply that. Besides, finding Alyssa would be the best thing I could do for my friend."

"That might be true Brian, but I don't know if you can be objective here. Now go commiserate with your buddy and let me do my job if you really want to find her."

I dismissed Brian and turned to Mr. Morelli "I have a team of investigators on their way to sweep the house. Also, I need the license plate number of the car she was driving?"

I met with little resistance from Morelli. He actually seemed relieved that I was taking action of some kind. If he thought what I was doing was fruitless, I am sure he would have been more resistant.

"I should know the plate number, but I can't tell you right off the top of my head, let me get it for you" Dante said as he walked to his office to retrieve the plate number.

As he walked away I concentrated my questioning to Mr. Martin. "So can you tell me again what time you last saw Mrs. Morelli?"

"Like I said earlier, she came in for almost exactly one hour and one hour only"

"Mr. Martin I'm merely trying to get a timeline so there is no need to get defensive"

"I understand Lieutenant, but you really don't have to sound so condescending" he replied as he walked away.

I started to follow Mr. Martin, as he was walking away, but stopped when the CSI team pulled into the driveway. I had more important things to tend to; therefore, I continued past the front door and met the team to quickly brief them on the situation at hand. "Hi Tom, Linda, how's it going?" As they got out of the car my eyes lighted first on Linda who was a petite blond with a great set of legs and a body to match. Tom looked like a typical lab rat. He might have been good looking had he not wore bottle cap glasses and dressed like he had slept in his clothes for days. He was habitually running his hands through his hair, which inevitably left it sticking up everywhere.

"Oh hanging in there. What do we have Mike?" Tom replied

"A predictable, missing female doctor last seen around 1:00 this afternoon, my gut tells me there is more here than meets the eye. Of course you guys are my eyes, so there can't be any fuck ups, because once you see who owns this house and who's wife it is you'll know it better be right from the get go. So everything goes by the book, nothing left unturned."

They nodded their approval. Linda frowned, "Why who owns it?"

"Take a look over your shoulder, coming out the front, lawyer in tow" I replied.

"She cursed under her breath. No way, is that Dante Morelli?"

"Jesus I would rather be anywhere but here. Thanks Senetti." Tom whispered.

"Hey we treat him like anyone else. Just do your jobs. Let's get started." I ordered feeling a little apprehensive myself.

"I will, but I have to say it makes me just a little nervous to know that he can just make me disappear if I don't do something right. On the other hand, if I do something right, I might disappear too. Either way this won't be good for anyone concerned." Tom complained.

"Let's start with the cars." I suggested, as I really don't think anything happened in the house." I was getting my gloves on when I noticed there were blood splatters on one car that was parked in the driveway in front of the CSI van. I called Tom over to get a sample before I asked whom the car belonged to.

"Tom can you come take a look at this?" I ordered as I pointed to an area near the rear passenger side door.

"This is fresh blood Senetti, like today, old/fresh, you can tell by the color it's started to clot… still red, not black yet" he answered after a cursory glance, "do you know whose car this is?" he asked as he got down to business taking pictures and swabbing the area for DNA.

"No, but I am going to find out" I replied, as I started to walk back towards the house.

"Excuse me, but can anyone tell me who owns the silver BMW outside?" I asked entering the house.

"That's my husband's new car. Do you need me to move it?" Dr. Martin replied.

"No, not just yet. Where did Mr. Martin go? I answered evasively as I walked purposefully into the center of the huge living room.

"I believe he's in the bathroom" Dr. Martin replied following me, nearly running to keep up. "Why?"

As I waited for Mr. Martin to come out of the restroom, I tried to piece things together. I wondered what Dr. Morelli was doing at Mr. Martin's office. If the Morelli's had such a good relationship why didn't Morelli have any idea that his wife was facing a malpractice suit? They seemed like a couple that had no secrets between them. There was something underlying all this that someone wasn't telling me.

No more had Mr. Martin opened the door than I confronted him. He had no choice but to back up into the bathroom a couple of steps. I shouldered my way into the room.

"Mr. Senetti?" he queried in surprise.

"Can you come with me outside, Mr. Martin?" I asked quietly. It was not so much a question as a command. I left him little choice.

"Sure, Senetti." He complied as we walked out of the house and neared his car with his wife still following closely behind.

"What's this all about Senetti?" Martin asked as he saw the crime team around his car.

"Well Mr. Martin we found some blood on the side of your passenger door and we are just investigating every option available to us, so is it ok for us to search your vehicle Mr. Martin?"

"You can't be serious Senetti. As a lawyer, I would never let you search my car without a warrant. I have confidential papers in that car. So my answer to you would be no."

"That won't be an issue Mr. Martin I can have a warrant down here pronto. You were the last person to see Alyssa Morelli. You have to admit that doesn't look so good." So either you can let us do our job or you can keep being a prick. I could give a shit about some papers that may deal with client/lawyer confidentiality, but I do care about getting to the truth behind Alyssa Morelli's disappearance. So, either way this car isn't going anywhere until we take a look at what's in it." I replied

"What does my car have to do with this investigation Senetti?" he asked sourly.

Before I had a chance to answer Morelli, who evidently got wind of our actions outside started to walk towards the area where we talking. Morelli had made all the right phone calls, because by the time I had finished my discussion with Mr. Martin there were half a dozen people getting out of cars and walking toward the house. Their demeanor left little doubt about their intentions.

"Senetti these men are private investigators that are here at your disposal. I know you might not want the help, but you are going to take it. Either that or get the fuck out of here and let me do things my way." Morelli said.

"Mr Morelli I think we have this under control. All these people will do is jeopardize any evidence that's here. So I need everyone here to back away and let the real police do their jobs." I replied so fucking irritated I wanted to strangle Morelli.

Morelli started talking to a few of the men that had showed up. They were guys you definitely didn't want to meet anywhere and you certainly didn't mess with them. Morelli spoke to them in low undertones that I couldn't make out, but fortunately they immediately turned on their heels and left. It seemed Morelli was playing by my rules for now.

But there was tension building. When I looked at him, he was always staring. And finally I guess he had about enough of the undercurrent and he strode toward me. I braced myself as he began. "What the hell is going on Senetti? Why are the monkeys hanging around Dave's car?" he demanded.

"They are looking at some blood drops that are on the side of my car, Dante" Dave answered. They want to look inside."

"Let them, so they can get on with things." said Morelli matter of fact.

"Yes Dave, why don't you just let us?" I chimed in. "I will have a warrant here in a couple of hours, but you could save a lot of time by giving us the go ahead. We will get what we want, with or without your cooperation. The car is going to be searched one way or another."

"Dave, what the hell is in there that is so important? We are talking about Alyssa here. I need to get things moving and the more time they waste with this shit about your car is an extra minute that

she isn't being found. So do me a huge favor AND OPEN THE
FUCKING DOOR AND LET THEM SEARCH!!!!"

"Fine Lieutenant, here are the keys, but my files are personal and
no judge would ever give a warrant for those. Take the car and if it
comes back to me with a single scratch on it there will be papers filed
with your name on it." he warned.

"Tom get a truck and move it to the garage now before this idiot
gets any other ideas. I want to see that car gone in the next fifteen
minutes." I said, finally feeling like Morelli and I were on the same
side.

"You got it Lt., we'll start the process." Tom replied.

"Linda, get everybody out of here and don't miss anything in or
around the domicile" I said satisfied that I was at last taking some
action.

"You sir." Linda replied.

I had a sinking feeling this wasn't going to end right for anybody
involved. Morelli would never find another night's rest if he truly
loved his wife. At this point I was inclined to believe he did. If he
finds out who took her before we do, God in heaven help them. Dave
was, at this point, the last person to see her alive and the thought
of it was nearly driving Morelli mad. It is obvious to me Morelli's
a man of suspicion. He is one of those men who trusts no one. He
can't sleep at night knowing that there is always someone out there
that wants what he has, and will get it by force if necessary. In this
case, it includes hitting his Achilles' heel, to get him through his
heart. . .Alyssa. In fact, I was thinking that might be the only way
to break the man, by hurting his wife. Morelli might never be the
same without her. In any case, this was not going to go down well.

As Morelli went back inside to get some of his belongings and
get me the information I needed, I followed him to his office to
get the license plate number. As he opened drawers to get me the
information, I noticed an older picture of Alyssa and Dante. I asked
where the picture was taken.

"It was taken on the first day we met" he replied as reached in
a desk as orderly as the rest of the house. "Here is the car and plate
information."

He handed me a few pages that came from his auto policy with
all the information I needed to get started on locating the car. As I

turned to leave, I looked back over my shoulder. For the first time I saw him weaken as he paused and stared at the picture. He sank in his desk chair with his hands to his forehead and his voice cracked when he asked if he could just have a few minutes.

"Sure Mr Morelli" I said as I closed the door softly, knowing this man never showed weakness.

CHAPTER 3

Dante - The Beginning

"*A*lyssa, Alyssa," walking into my office she is all I can think about through the fog in my head. I look at the picture on my desk taken the night we met. I hold it to my chest as I remember the incredible coincidence that would entangle my life with this incredible woman. It seems like yesterday that I remember seeing her for the first time. . . .

It was February 18, 1986 and I was just having a glass of Merlot and perusing the menu at Montecatinni's Restaurant when I noticed a woman across the room walking in my direction. I could tell she was giving me a serious once over and liked what she saw. I was still dressed in a black Hugo Boss suit with a white shirt and red tie. She smiled, and I couldn't quit looking at her. If I thought she was beautiful before, when she smiled she dazzled me. I caught my breath as she boldly walked up to my table. It wasn't until later I found out she thought I was the blind date she was supposed to meet.

"So mister, are you ready for me?" she asked as she pulled out the chair opposite me and started to sit down.

My words caught in my throat, "excuse me". I was thinking I was the luckiest son of a bitch in the place, but my face obviously registered confusion.

"Oh my God, let me guess you are not Allen." She was the one flustered now.

"Sorry sweetheart, I don't even look like an Allen, but I can be an Allen if you stay in that chair. Hell I can be whoever you want me to be."

She gave a nervous laugh, and I loved that laugh from the first time I heard it. It was melodious like the trill of a piano. "I am so sorry I confused you with someone I am supposed to meet here."

"That's fine I was only going to eat, but eating can wait. In fact it can wait forever." I said. Something about her made me feel young and happy inside, there were definitely sparks. I felt an immediate connection that made me say ridiculous things. I was usually very reserved and habitually sarcastic and here I was making a fool out of myself.

She smiled apologetically "I am so sorry to bother you. I really did think you were my blind date, maybe I was just hoping you were." She got up regretfully.

As she walked away I tried to go back to the business of ordering, but eating was the last thing on my mind. She was really something. I tried to think about what it was about her that made her different from all the other women I had been with. She had a special way about her. She wasn't just any typical woman by anybody's standards, but there was something, what was it? Chemistry! I hoped that fate would let me see this woman again.

I got up, leaving a nearly uneaten dinner wondering how someone like that could walk in and out of my life so quickly. As I was getting up to leave I couldn't help but notice that she was eating alone. There was no lucky bastard sitting across from her. Quietly, on my way out I asked the Maitre D' to put her bill on my tab and to make sure she had the best. Again fate took a hand and she turned to look at the door where her date was supposed to materialize. Our eyes met across the room. I took a deep breath, took a chance and walked back, just to say goodbye I told myself, but instead of a farewell, my natural cockiness took over,

"Are you ready for me?"

She laughed and asked me if I would like to help her finish a nice bottle of Arottzins. My eyes widened in surprise, what are the chances that she'd be drinking my favorite wine?

"How could I refuse good wine and beautiful company," I replied smoothly, even though my insides were churning. I introduced myself "My name is Dante Morelli and your name is?" I reached my hand across the table to shake hers. Her slender hand felt strong and warm inside of mine. I held on maybe a moment too long, but truth is I never wanted to let go.

"Alyssa Mathews" she answered again flashing me her brilliant smile. "I don't know what kind of wine you like, but we can order something else." She was stammering and I knew then that she was just as nervous as I was.

I tried to ease her discomfort as well as my own. "You are drinking my favorite wine. Why else do you think I came back?" I teased.

"Oh I don't know. I thought it might be because you just couldn't resist me." She said, as she tossed her hair coquettishly to one side.

Her banter was closer to the truth than she realized. "Well that might have something to do with it." I countered." And I just had to find out why a woman as gorgeous as you would go on a blind date. I'm sure you could have a date with any man alive."

"Thanks for that, even though I know all you were interested in is my wine" she laughed then sobered, "but it's rather a long tiresome story."

I looked at my watch "I think I have the time, take all night if you want." I stared at her beauty, watching her talk was mesmerizing. The way her mouth smiled, her lips sparkled....those lips.....what I could...... Stop it I told myself. Listen to her...but damn I loved her teeth, her mouth, her lips … I wanted to touch....

"Are you with me or am I boring you before I even start" Alyssa brought me back abruptly.

"I'm sorry I was just staring at your mouth." I blurted truthfully, kicking myself for being so blunt. "I'm here and I'm listening. Go on."

"Ok, well, I'm here looking at programs where I can do my residency. Since my friend Ellen is from here she decided to set me up with her friend Allen whom I will never forgive for standing me up."

"I forgive him. In fact I damn near love him." I said.

She laughed and blushed just a little. "I will have to admit I'm liking Allen better all the time."

"Not too much I hope."

"Let's just say he won't get a second chance. But I will have to thank him for standing me up."

"Yeah, me too. So tell me Miss Alyssa Matthews where are you from?

"A small town in Maine called Cape Elizabeth. I doubt you have ever heard of it.

"No can't say that I have, but sounds nice. All of those small towns have their own unique character."

"You said you were looking for a residency here, in what?"

"Psychiatry."

"Wow a doctor! I'm impressed. I didn't know they made pretty doctors. I thought psychiatrists were at least sixty and looked very stern and stuffy."

"Sorry to disappoint you Mr. Morelli."

"I'm not disappointed I assure you. But I better be careful or you'll be analyzing me and that would not be a good thing"

"OK, your turn, so Mr. Messelli what's your story?

"It's Morelli with an r." I smiled praying she liked my smile half as much as I liked hers.

"What you see is not what you get." I work for my father as a Financial Consultant and handle most of the day-to-day operations for Morelli Inc. I live in the North Beach District in San Francisco. I went to business school at Stanford University where I received my MBA. I am currently single and my blood type is red."

"Well my blood type is also red so now we have something in common. I am currently finishing Med. school at the University of Pennsylvania and as I said I'm specializing in psychiatry" she offered.

"Smart and beautiful your parents must be proud of you."

"Well my dad is and my mom would be but she," she faltered for a moment, "she passed away,"

"I'm sorry I said, I can tell you still hurt."

"Well I don't know why I'm telling you this, but "her eyes looked troubled," my mom committed suicide I think that's what made me choose psychiatry. I talk to my dad every few days to check up on him and make sure he is ok. We are pretty close. In fact, I would have to say my dad is the most important man in my life."

"I hope he is the only man in your life. And by the way I think your career choice is admirable."

"Actually he is, yes. I am an only child so I'm pretty much the center of his universe as well, so I keep close tabs on him. How about you, any brothers or sisters?"

"Two older sisters that might as well have been my mother. They are very over protective I have a great family, they love all my faults and me so, that's all I can ask for. One owns a nice Café in the Sunset and the other is happily married and lives in Marin County and thoroughly loves being a housewife."

We talked and drank wine for the remainder of the night, filling each other in on our lives. I felt comfortable with her as if we had known each other forever. I was amazed at how easy I could speak to her. I've been with women, lots of women, but really talked to few. My entire life I have been close mouthed. She was in all truth a complete stranger and yet she made me feel at ease like no one ever had. And I was flying. As I talked and listened, I felt like I was in grade school and I was going through my first crush. I had that silly, crazy feeling that made my face hurt from smiling. I couldn't remember ever feeling like I was grinning on the inside.

I didn't want the night to end, but the maître d came to our table and said "we are closing Mr. Morelli."

"Let me guess you own the place?" she asked quizzically.

"No it's just one of my favorite spots to eat. I'm a regular here, that's all. I didn't notice we were the only ones left. I had no idea it was that late." I said regretfully.

"Well I guess we should go before they throw us out, but would you take a picture with me so I can tell all my friends this is the person I made an ass out of myself in front of" she giggled.

"Sure" I waved over the maître d to take the picture. "John old boy, if you want to get me out of here and close this joint, you'll have to take a picture of us."

He grinned. "Sure thing Mr. Morelli." We leaned in close to each other and he snapped the picture. "What a beautiful couple you make Mr. Morelli." he said.

"Thanks buddy." I said reminding myself to tip him handsomely. As stodgy as he seemed he was quite a romantic. "OK we'll get out of your way. Take care. See you soon." And he smiled when he saw the tip I had added on to the bill.

As we got up together I wrapped her coat around her shoulders and asked if I could see her again.

"Sorry, but I'm flying back to Pennsylvania in the morning. Here's my number. I would like it very much if we kept in touch." she said hopefully.

As I walked her to her car and opened the door for her, she reached over and kissed my cheek and said "Good night Dante it was a pleasure meeting you and for the record, I am going to send Allen a thank you card."

It was a moment I will never forget. The light touch of her lips on my cheek turned my blood hot. I couldn't understand my reaction to the briefest flutter of lips on my cheek. This woman had an amazing affect on me. I didn't want her to go. I knew in a moment that I wanted her. I wanted her to be in my life every hour of every day. I craved her. I knew this could easily be called an obsession. I had never truly fallen for any woman. There were times I thought I had been in love, but it was nothing like this. I had to have this woman. I wanted her.

"Cool it Dante" I told myself. "Back off!"

A few days went by, but I still couldn't forget her. It wasn't just her beauty that dazzled me. She touched my heart. I couldn't explain the longing. I kept fighting myself. Should I call her? Had she forgotten me? Did she feel the same? The damn questions tormented me. I felt like a teenager, insecure and afraid of being turned down. This wasn't how I behaved with women. I was in control. They wanted me. I was sure and easy and suave. I decided I couldn't keep going on like this. I had to find out if she cared for me. I decided to fly to Philadelphia to surprise her. I was tired of mooning around like a schoolboy.

My first step was to do a little investigating. I found out where she lived. I bought a ticket and took a quick flight. It was so unlike me to do something like this in the middle of a week. After flying in I booked a hotel room and found a florist's shop and had them send some flowers. On the card I had the florist write "thank you for an unforgettable evening" and sign my name. I waited until the delivery boy called me to let me know my flowers had been delivered then dialed the number she had given me. As the phone rang I marveled that a man like me could be brought to the level of a love sick puppy.

Two rings then "hello." God it was good to hear her voice again.

"Alyssa?" I asked, knowing it was.

"Yes." she answered softly.

"Hi Alyssa. I don't know if you remember me. This is Dante from California. We met a few days ago at a restaurant called Montecatinni's"

"Dante….. hmm….. Dante nope can't say that I do. Wait was that the guy with the lazy eye, limp and pot belly?" She started laughing.

"Very funny." I laughed back feeling all warm and happy inside.

"Remember you, of course I remember you as if I could forget. I just received your flowers and they are beautiful, thank you. But to tell you the truth I would have liked them more if you had given them to me in person. And what took you so long to call? I was beginning to think you had forgotten all about me."

"Not to sound repetitive, but how could I forget? And as for delivering them in person, if I can come over I'll bring you another dozen."

"Where are you?"

"I am at the Ritten House Hotel. I have to tell you I think your five star hotels are comparable to California."

"In Philadelphia??!"

"Of course. You are going to think this is strange, and I don't want you to think I am some kind of nut or something, but I couldn't stop thinking of that night we met. Just the thought of you made me smile. So, I figured "What the hell, jump on a plane and go see her.""

"I was hoping you'd say something like that. It was a memorable night and to be honest with you I really was hoping you'd call."

"So do you have any plans for the night?"

"Yes I do… when are you picking me up?"

"I can be there in about an hour, but since it's your city you decide what we do"

"Deal, see you an about an hour, let me give you the address."

"I have it already remember I sent flowers"

"Oh that's right, well in an hour then."

As she hung up the phone I let out a sigh of relief. She felt the same. I felt like dancing, instead I went around my hotel room getting ready smiling a silly smile the whole time. I was happy that I was going to see her again and beyond that nothing else mattered. I knew this was more than fate, more than a chance encounter. This was the real thing. I could feel it. I was not only very fond of this woman I had met in California, I was falling in love, really in love for the first time in my life. No woman had ever made me want to drop everything and get on a plane just to see her. The anticipation was unbearable. I didn't know if I could wait an entire hour. So, I finished getting ready, called a taxi, bought another bouquet of flowers and headed to her place.

Just then a knock interrupted my daydream, bringing me back to the present nightmare. I looked back down at the picture taken that first night and held it to my chest for a moment, then I carefully put it back on my desk, and called "Come in."

CHAPTER 4

Senetti –Suspicions Arise

"Sorry to bother you Mr. Morelli, but we have to get started on the house." I said

"Sure and here is the most recent picture of her. It was taken last week at a fundraiser for the hospital where she volunteers." He replied.

As Dante stepped out of the room, all the negative things I had ever heard of him made me innately suspicious. He wasn't known to be a legal player in the game of life. He was a powerful figure with a status and that made him extremely dangerous. Could the possibility of getting to Alyssa be the angle here? Did he fall out of love with her or she with him? Was he having an affair or was she? There were many plausible motives, and the most obvious place to begin was with Morelli.

I left the team to collect what they could. I didn't think there would be much, but I couldn't rule out anything. The clock was ticking and I needed to find Alyssa Morelli, because every hour that slipped by left a slimmer chance that she would be found alive, so I called in a favor.

I phoned my friend Morgan Hoffman at the local television station to request her help.

"Hi Morgan this is Mike from Missing Persons," I said.

"Oh hi Mike what's up? I'm pretty sure you didn't call to chit chat."

"Listen, I need a favor for your ten o'clock."

"Sure Mike what can I help with? she asked.

"Well I'm perusing a missing person and it's urgent. It's Alyssa Morelli, Dante Morelli's wife. She has been missing since this afternoon. It's getting close to eight hours since anyone saw her."

"Oh my god Mike where are you right now. This is huge," she gasped.

"I am at the Morelli residence and will be for a while longer. I can have someone bring you a picture of her and the information on the vehicle she was driving. I would like to get the word out to see if someone has seen her or her car" I said.

"I go on in forty-five minutes if you want to have someone drive down the photos. Mike, also I would like an exclusive with you, since you owe me for this one, I want to be kept in the loop." She said.

"I will do what I can, but let's keep this open as a missing person bulletin for right now. I know how the media can put a spin on things." I said

"Sounds good, I will be waiting for the information. Have someone drop it off immediately to the front desk and to my attention. I will talk to you in a little while. Bye. Oh and Mike thanks. This helps me as much as it helps you."

I knew that if I got the word out to masses through the media I would have a better chance to get some information, for instance: Where she was last seen? Has anyone seen her car? Did someone see something; hell anything at this point would be a blessing?

"Linda" I called out. "Can you do me a favor and run this picture down to Channel 2 KTVU, Attention: Morgan Hoffman. We are going to go live with this." I said.

"Sure thing Lt. I can go right now." Linda replied

At this point I had to tell Morelli what I was doing. I knew he wasn't going to like the attention, but I also knew if this woman was alive this was the best way to make sure she stayed that way. Walking back to the front of the house where everyone was conversing, I interrupted to let them know a missing person bulletin was going to be aired in less than an hour.

"That is excellent Mr. Senetti, I have been calling everyone that we know, hoping someone has heard from her or seen her" Ellen said "but so far haven't had any luck."

"No damn media circus in my house you hear me Senetti." Dante spit out.

"It's not going to be like that Mr. Morelli. This is just a bulletin asking for help finding her. I sent the picture you gave me with the car information. My hope is someone will call and say they have seen her somewhere or they have seen the car. Then, we can start getting a better timeline. Also, I am going to need her cell phone number in order to start tracing all calls to and from that phone. I will make the necessary calls and get all the man power available in this search." I said

Dante immediately softened. I could tell he wasn't thinking of the media attention that would be focused on him, but was thinking of what might find his wife when he said, "Thank you for all your help, I really do appreciate it."

"I'm just doing my job, which means finding your wife and finding her alive. Time is of the optimum importance right now. There really isn't an alternative you understand."

"I do." He whispered. He looked like a man that was hurting beyond belief. The pain showed in his eyes and his powerful body seemed haggard. Either Dante Morelli was a great actor or his feelings were indeed genuine. But then I chastised myself, who was I kidding, this is Dante Morelli a man with no conscience; a killer, a ruthless business man with no scruples. Word in the city was that if anyone crossed him then that person ends up missing. So my concern for Alyssa was that this woman hadn't just done a disappearing act at the hands of Dante Morelli.

I headed downtown to the office to get ready for the briefing. I could only hope the ten o'clock news flash would come up with some helpful leads. I felt as haggard as Morelli looked. It had been a long night and it was only going to get longer. I grabbed some much-needed caffeine from the never empty pot in the lounge and hurried to my little shithole of an office to watch the coverage. As I looked up to the small television set that was hanging above me in my little cubicle I prayed I had done the right thing and that this would go well.

"Good Evening this is Michael Bradburry"

"And I am Morgan Hoffman. We start tonight with breaking news: a missing prominent, San Francisco woman Dr. Alyssa Morelli. She is a well-known psychiatrist in the San Francisco area and wife of well-known business tycoon Dante Morelli. The police have found little to go on and are appealing to the public for help. Her full name is Alyssa Fay Morelli, she is 39 years old; she has light brown hair and hazel eyes; she weighs around 135 and is 5 foot 8 inches. She was last seen wearing a blue pinstriped suit this afternoon at approximately one o'clock in the Market District. She drives a white Mercedes Benz SL 500.This is a recent photo that you are now seeing posted." In the corner of the screen the picture Dante had given me popped up. "Please look at it carefully. Law enforcement officials are counting on the public to come forward if there is any information concerning this highly respected woman. So, if anyone sees Doctor Morelli or her vehicle please call San Francisco Police Department at 415-555-1212.

"Do we know if there are any leads?" Bradburry asked.

"What we know right now is what the police are telling us, which isn't very much unfortunately." Hoffman replied.

"Do investigators think her disappearance might have something to do with Mr. Morelli's business dealings?" Bradburry pursued.

"Again, Micheal," Morgan answered stiffly, showing her obvious displeasure with this line of questioning,"from what I understand, the police have very little to go on, that's why they are going public with this." She smiled tightly at him with only her mouth, but her eyes warned him of her disapproval. "And we move to other breaking news…" and Senetti turned the volume down to merely background noise.

"God damn it." Senetti cursed.

"What's up Senetti?" another officer asked poking his head around the door.

"Ahh these damn reporters always trying to make more of something that's not there yet." Senetti grumbled as he grabbed his jacket off the back of the chair and headed to the elevator. Just as he started to push the down arrow, a voice came from behind him.

"Hey Lieutenant."

"Hey Morris" Senetti replied.

"Man I just heard the news, and I also heard you're on this one. Need any help?" Morris asked hopefully, looking like an ad for the All-American Boy with his clean-cut hair, blue eyes, and dimples that showed when he gave you a bright white smile.

Senetti, sighed. Morris was a good kid, he had the makings of a great investigator, but he just didn't have experience. He was a young, new homicide detective, so for him to step up to the plate and ask to give me a hand, I couldn't refuse, knowing that I could be over my head here and I could use someone younger than me to do all the running around. So, what the hell, might as well help the rookie. "Well this isn't a homicide yet Morris, but if you want to start getting your feet wet, you can help me out by starting to look up any dirt on these people you can find, and I assure you there is plenty on Dante Morelli, but nothing the law has ever been able to make stick. He is one bright SOB."

Morris nearly danced with anticipation. "Yes sir. I'm on it sir."

"Whoa slow down. There is one condition; you only answer to me and don't tell anyone anything else that you find or that we talk about, since these fucking walls seem to have ears." Here's the info I have so far, take a look at my notes and start digging.

"No problem Lt. Let me tell my sergeant that I am working this one with you for now and get it cleared." He was nearly skipping, but turned around, "and thanks Senetti." Morris said beaming.

"For what?"

"For letting me work with you, especially on this case." Morris said, as he jogged down the hallway.

"Don't start thanking me yet. This is going to get dirty as hell if we don't find this woman." I yelled after his retreating back.

As I got into the elevator to head home for some much-needed sleep, I recapped all that had happened. I couldn't stop thinking about a couple of comments that Dante made.

"She never keeps anything from me." Yet he also said "She never said anything about a malpractice suit." The duplicity of these two statements struck me. Why hadn't she told Dante? Had it slipped her mind? Wasn't it important? Was it too insignificant to bother him about? Who was going to file the lawsuit against her? Shit...my head ached with a million unanswered questions. And yet I couldn't turn it off. My mind wandered to Dave. I couldn't overlook him, since he was after all the last person to see her that afternoon. Yet why would he even offer that info. if he did anything wrong? And I certainly couldn't overlook DANTE MORELLI the biggest asshole in the city. I'm sure there are plenty of people that would want to see him taken down, because if you ask nearly anyone Dante Morelli is considered untouchable.

I wearily climbed in my car and started my drive home. I couldn't stop thinking of this woman that I had never met. From all accounts she was a very beautiful, accomplished woman, so why would anyone want to harm her. Everything pointed to Dante or someone going after Dante through her, but I've been wrong before, but instinct told that someone I had talked to, someone close to her, was involved in her disappearance.

Just as I pulled in my driveway, and turned off the ignition my damn radio started to go off.

"Senetti you there?" The Dispatcher asked.

God I wanted to ignore the question, go in my house and sleep for days, but instead I answered "Senetti here."

"Linda and Tom from CSI want you in the garage as soon as you can get there."

"It's 1:45 in the morning can it wait till later? Can't they call me on my Nokia?" I said.

"Just a minute, let me ask them and I will give you a holler back." she said

I sat hesitantly in my car, never moving from behind the wheel, I knew what the answer was going to be

"They said it's urgent Lt. and it's something you should see for yourself.," the dispatcher said

"Yeah I am in my car. Let them know that I will be there in about thirty-five minutes you copy that dispatch?"

"Copy that"

Damn, just when I thought I was going to get some rest. I started back to the garage. What on earth could be so important that they needed me tonight? I knew it had to be crucial since they wouldn't tell me over the radio. Still my mind was racing to find out what it was.

CHAPTER 5

Senetti - Evidence

I drove off the Bay Bridge to make my right onto Bryant to get to the police station where Dave Martin's car had been towed. I was greeted by at least a dozen media vans who had already beat me to the sight, waiting to pounce for their next bit of news. I drove to the back door radioing Morris to let me in so I could avoid the horde of reporters.

As I got out of my car Linda met me on the run talking as she ushered me into the building. "Holy Shit Senetti. You are not going to believe what we found when we searched the car." Linda chattered.

"So spill it and let's get this night over with" I said exhausted, yet I felt the adrenaline start pumping as her excitement was infectious and my curiosity got the better of my lack of sleep.

"I'll wait 'til we get to the garage and let Tom tell you since he found what we both think you will find interesting." Linda replied as we walked down the cold cinder block hallways of 850 Bryant. I could see more and more agents gathering at the entrance of the of the CSI garage.

"What the hell is going on here? Everyone get back to work." They started to scatter. I grabbed Morris by the arm "Morris you stay here, so we can catch up on all this together. I would hate to have to go over this again." I said.

"Not a problem." Morris replied, with that feverish anticipation in his eyes.

"Well I think we found some evidence that gives us a plausible first suspect in this missing case." Linda said.

I had, had enough of the drama. "Enough of the suspense, what the hell are you talking about?" I questioned.

"Hey Senetti." Tom said as he crawled from under Dave Martin's BMW. "Either this Dave Martin is a complete idiot, which as a lawyer doesn't seem believable, or he is being setup and I mean really set up." Tom said crawling out from under the car.

I cut him off "I don't want a parade of people here, so let's go to the CSI lab and talk."

We started back to the CSI lab area where we sat down in the conference room to put everything on the table. "Alright so where do you want to start?" I asked.

Tom didn't give anyone a chance to talk, he charged right in "Man there are so many angles here I don't know where to begin."

"Why don't you start with the obvious, the blood" I said with a hint of irritation.

"Well just like we thought, the blood splatter isn't very old. We took a swab and sent it in for DNA analysis. We also received Mrs. Morelli's blood donor sheet, which tells us her blood type, it matches the type on Dave Martin's car. And there is more. When we did a sweep of the Morelli house and found her hair strands on a couple of brushes and in her sink. We took those as well as some of her personal belongings that might have some of her DNA to run a comparability check.

"She lived there of course there's hair. Why take some of her hair? Unless you are telling me you found her hair in the car."

Tom answered, "That's exactly what I am telling you. And the hair sample's we found still had the hair bulb."

Sometimes these guys pissed me off. What the hell was a hair bulb. They acted as if I should know all this shit. "And so....this means what?" I asked exasperated.

"It means the hair in the car probably had to have been pulled out by force not just by falling out. Those strands from the car also showed stretching indicating again they where pulled out. We have a person that is great with hair analysis. She should be here this morning to take a look." Here Tom paused "I am saving the best for last." He said drawing it out.

The guy was good at what he did, but damn it his flair for the theatrical in holding out the information was making my already short fuse ready to explode "Fucking get to it Tom." I said exasperated.

"Ok Ok.." He was finally getting the point that I couldn't tolerate one single second more of his bullshit. "We also brushed the car for fingerprints and we found her fingerprints in the back of the car. We saw the index finger on the passenger side window and a palm print on the doorknob…it seemed to indicate she was getting out or at the very least had grabbed the doorknob, from the angle it looked as if she were in a reclining position. What makes this interesting is there is no blood on the inside; however, there are also fingerprints on the outside and those prints overlapped the blood splatter we found earlier at Morelli's house. If that is indeed her blood, which was type B+ and her blood type, she was there when the blood hit the door and prints indicated that her hand not only hit the car door, but some of the blood splatters were slightly smeared downward, showing the prints came on top of, or after the blood."

I was overwhelmed for a minute, then I said "This is all amazing, but how do you know they were Alyssa Morelli's fingerprints?"

Linda chuckled, "Well guess what, the good doctors Ellen Martin and Alyssa Morelli were evidently party girls in college. Both their fingerprints were in the database. They were arrested for pot and get this, indecent exposure."

I raised my eyebrows "Now that's two babes I would like to see exposed," I laughed. "Please go on."

"Well it's not all as exciting as that, but it seems the ladies smoked a bit of pot and decided to flash the nerds in the adjoining dorms, or something to that effect according to the reports. The RA on their floor saw them in the window from the sidewalk below and turned them into campus security. The campus cops went up to their room and found more than naked girls, they found pot and alcohol, so the city cops were called and an arrest was made. It didn't go any further than a fine, but it was enough to get their fingerprints on file.

I had to organize the information I had just heard. I picked up the dry erase marker and started listing the evidence on the board. In huge letters I printed the word timeline at the top. I put 12:00 on the board….Alyssa showed at Martin's office for malpractice suit. She leaves at 1:00. …Corroborated by secretary….Morris piped up "Wait

I called Martin's secretary at home this evening. She said she saw Alyssa come in at 12:00, but the secretary left for lunch, as was usual, at 12:00. She said that Mrs. Morelli was gone before the secretary got back at 1:00. However, when she got back Mr. Martin's 1:00 o'clock appointment was waiting and she buzzed Mr. Martin who told her to send them in, in about five minutes.

"Good work." I said. I was impressed with young Morris's initiative. "This leaves us an hour window, when Dave Martin could have conceivably killed Alyssa Morelli. I turned back to the timeline. I wrote 1:00 to 4:00 …appointments were kept as corroborated by secretary. I looked to Morris who eagerly shook his head in agreement. I added the time 4:45 to the board and wrote Dante Morelli calls in missing wife.

Linda said, "That doesn't tell us where Dave Martin was the last hour of the day either."

Tom added "Well for that matter where was Dante from 1:00 to 4:45."

Morris said, "I'll check the parking slips to see when or if Dave's car left the garage."

"Thanks Morris" I said really appreciating him and glad I had brought him aboard.

Then Dave threw out a few more thoughts "What time did Dave show up at the Morelli house? When does he get off work? And what time did Ellen call him? Did he leave immediately?"

Again Morris offered… "I'll check the phone records on the call."

"Well I got there at 5:30 and Dave didn't get there 'til about 5:45. I don't know what time he left the office or if he was at the office when Ellen called him? Which number did she call?" I asked.

Morris wrote on his notepad and answered "I will get those phone records when I get the others."

We all just looked at the timeline. There were still so many possibilities….Dante….Dave some unknown entity….. "Well I said in order to rule out Dave, Linda get a hold of Judge Plantz; he is usually quicker to issue a warrant than anyone else. We have enough for a search warrant for the Martin's house, but it's a little early for a warrant. If anyone will give us one, it will be Plantz. He will give it to you before he will us Linda because you look better in short, tight skirts than we do." I winked at her as she grimaced. After Linda gets the warrant, Tom head up the search and call me when you get something, same with you Morris. Now all of you leave me the hell alone, 'cuz I'm going home to get a few hours sleep.

Tom and Linda got up to do the jobs I had assigned. I again cautioned them "don't speak to anyone about this case. Take what you get and discuss it here, but do not, and I mean do not, give it to the media or even to anyone else in the department."

Linda said "Lt. we have to trust someone."

"Yeah and that someone is me; so it goes nowhere."

Tom and Linda got up and started to trudge down the hall. Morris sidled next to me, somehow knowing I needed to talk to him. I asked Morris if he was sure he wanted in on this. Things were not only complicated, but could get dangerous. "Your career could be on the line, because in a case like this politics are always involved. I don't want to disillusion you, because I remember what it was like to be young. I wanted to save the world once too. But I'm telling you, there is corruption even in law enforcement. I can guarantee you that Morelli and who knows, even Dave Martin, have paid snitches in this department. You remind me of when I was your age and I hope you don't end up bitter or jaded, but you have to know the truth or you will jeopardize everything you believe and stand for. I've learned to pick my battles, but there have been some that will plague me forever. This is one of the battles where there won't be a winner. Now I'm asking you again are you in or out. You can walk away now if you want."

He said what I knew he would without a moment's hesitation "I'm in." then he added "'til death do us part Senetti."

"Ok then let's get to work. We need to notify Dave and Ellen Martin and after that Dante Morelli. After Linda has the search warrant we bring all three separately in for questioning. We will bring in the Martins first starting with Dave, since he was the last to see her alive, then find out just what Ellen knows and what kind of relationship they all had, then after we hear what the Martins have to say, we will bring in Dante Morelli."

Morris nodded his headed enthusiastically.

I nearly collapsed from exhaustion. I needed to go to my office and sift through everything again, but I needed just a couple hours of sleep. Worse I knew if Plantz granted the warrants they would be in soon, so there was no sense in going home. Morris was more observant than I thought. "Senetti go grab a few hours sleep. I'm on this and you know I will let you know the minute we find anything." I nodded and stumbled to my desk to lay my head down, hoping I could stop my brain for just an hour or so.

CHAPTER 6

Dave – The Inquisition Begins

$\mathcal{I}$ watched apprehensively as Morris and his counterpart, Senetti, pull up to our home in a four door cruiser. Morris climbed out of the passenger side and rang the bell. It really came as no surprise, I had been expecting to be questioned; however, I wasn't expecting the two CSI vans that pulled up behind them.

I let him wait for a few minutes before answering out of pure obstinacy, and truthfully I was a little scared of the man. When I opened the door, Morris told me I was wanted for questioning down at the precinct and the CSI teams had a warrant to search the house.

I took the warrant and skimmed it as Senetti came up to the door. "I can't imagine how you got a judge to grant this warrant." I said as I read. Then I saw evidence listed. "This is bull-shit." I sputtered. "Oh Jesus this is a fucking set-up. Alyssa wasn't anywhere near my car. We met in my office." I clamped my mouth shut. I was a lawyer I knew better than to say anything.

Senetti said, "You and your wife are coming downtown for questioning.

I was still reeling, but had collected myself and answered in my courtroom voice "Why Senetti, you know I am a lawyer, it's a waste of time?"

"You still need to show. Finish your coffee, better yet, I'll give you a cup there."

Ellen came up behind me, I could feel her hand on my shoulder "let's go Dave we need to do anything we can to help find Alyssa." She looked tired this morning and I knew she was worried, as was I, but all I could think about was the list of evidence, "blood", "hair", "fingerprints".

We rode in silence to the station. She took my hand, but I found no comfort there. Truth was, I knew things hadn't been good between us in a long time.

We walked into the station to the interrogation room. The metal chairs seemed cold and impersonal. I had been here before with clients, but never expected to find myself in this position. True to his word Senetti did send a flunky to get me a cup of coffee. Senetti spieled off my rights. I said, "Call my lawyer."

"Fine." Senetti answered. "I figured as much. Bring Ellen in."

"She will be represented as well," I said walking out of the room.

"I what?" Ellen heard me. "I don't need a lawyer. I just want to find my best friend, what the hell Dave. Can't we just for once forget the legal shit and quit wasting time. I'm so afraid for her. For God sakes you know we have nothing to hide."

"Even innocent people need lawyers." I answered even knowing as I did that once again I would give in to her demands. She ordered… I complied.

"I'll go first" she told Senetti.

He shrugged, but unlike everyone else who did what she told them, he said "Thanks for support, but I prefer to speak to your husband first."

She looked taken back; few ever disagreed with my wife, especially men. She was a beautiful woman, a talented, gorgeous woman. Her skills as a plastic surgeon made other women still wish they looked like her after going under her knife. She never took no for an answer, but she wore the pants in the family and everyone, including me, knew it. However, Senetti gave her no choice and I felt a brief moment of juvenile satisfaction that she hadn't gotten her way.

Senetti looked at me and I gave in, once again a pushover, but hey if anyone can get the better of my wife, no matter how insignificant the situation, I will follow him. So, against my better judgment I followed Senetti back into the room.

Senetti handed me the cup of luke warm coffee and again ran through my Miranda Rights. I sat down. Senetti pushed the button on the recorder to stop it, and then he looked me in the eyes and said, "Off the record I don't think you did this. I know you aren't stupid enough to do what we have found." Either the guy truly believed in me, or he was damn good at his job, but I found myself believing him.

So, still being cautious and using all my faculties as a lawyer I said, "Ok go."

Senetti pushed the button, he began with all the preliminaries."My name is Lt. Mike Senetti. It is 8:45AM on the 19th of March, 1997. Mr. Martin, you were the last to see Alyssa Morelli, will you tell us what transpired that day."

Again I thought carefully about all I was going to say and I began haltingly. "As I told you yesterday, Alyssa called me for a consultation."

Senetti interrupted, "What time did she call you?"

"It was after 9:00. You can check with my secretary, she has a call log and can give you the exact time."

Senetti nodded, "Go ahead."

"Well she said she had a malpractice suit pending and wanted some advice. I had appointments scheduled all day, as did she, but she suggested maybe we could meet over lunch. For anyone else I wouldn't have done it, but for Alyssa I said yes."

"What time did she show then?" Senetti asked.

"Alyssa is always on time, if not early, so it was probably a bit before 12:00. Again my secretary would know."

"The conversation then?" Senetti prompted.

"She never disclosed the client, but explained the situation. All I can tell you she was being threatened with a malpractice suit. I can't tell you specifics, because then I'm breaching lawyer/client confidentiality as you know."

"You said threatened." Senetti sat up alert. "Was she frightened? Did her husband know about this individual?"

"If you know Dante Morelli, you know she couldn't tell him about a client, let alone a client that in any way would harm his wife."

"Ok" Senetti said, "I can see that. Now tell me. Did anyone else see the two of you together?"

I thought for a moment "Just my secretary Kathy Moore."

"When did she leave your office?"

"I looked at my clock at 12:50 and as much as I hated to, knew we had to wrap it up, because we both had 1:00 o'clock appointments, so she had to have left shortly before that. Mrs. Moore came in after that to tell me my one o'clock was waiting. I asked her to give me a few minutes and then to show them in."

"A few minutes….why?"

"I needed to prepare myself."

Senetti's eyebrows rose questioningly.

"I had to brief myself on their legal status" I explained seeing where his thoughts might be going.

"Did your one o'clock see Alyssa leave?"

"I would assume so, since we didn't get started 'til after 1:00 and my secretary had to have seen Alyssa leave as well."

"And who was your 1:00 o'clock?"

"A litigation team that we contract for depositions."

"You finished with them at what time?"

"They left at 4:00 and then I finished my dictations for the day with my secretary about 5:00. I was still with my secretary and just wrapping up when my wife called with the information about Alyssa. You can again verify it with my secretary."

Senetti replied, "Well here's the deal Mr. Martin. We have talked to your secretary. She has corroborated everything. We know Alyssa Morelli called your office at 9:15. We know she showed at 11:55. What we don't know was when she left or if you indeed stayed in your office for the entire hour or even for that matter what you did in your office, since this seems to be more of a friend helping a friend. Your secretary tells us there is no legal documentation. We will be issuing a search warrant for your office. You see your secretary left at 12:00 after Alyssa entered your office. She said she left as usual for lunch. She came back at 1:00 and let you know your 1:00 o'clock was waiting. She did not however see Alyssa leave your office."

I looked at him incredulously…the evidence was overwhelming… no one saw her leave my office….. as a lawyer the full impact hit me. No fucking witnesses….even worse than the law…..Dante probably already knew…. no one saw his wife leave my office.

I felt myself blanch as Senetti continued. "You saw the evidence on the warrant. We found blood, hair and fingerprints on and in your vehicle. The fingerprints have already been confirmed and it's only a matter of time before the DNA results come back to confirm hair and blood samples. As he pushed over the evidence jacket he said, "You're a bright man, and this isn't looking good for you from my perspective.

Barely audible I whispered,…"I need my attorney." I couldn't even think about his perspective. I thought about Dante Morelli's perspective.

CHAPTER 7

Ellen-The Interview's Continue

I sat tiredly waiting for Dave to come out. I decided to go to the lounge to get a cup of coffee hoping to be more alert. As I walked in the lounge, I saw the young detective, Morris, leave the observation room. He was on his phone. "Linda, hit Plantz up for another search warrant. Yeah we need one for Dave Martin's office." I heard as he rounded the corner and I lost the end of the conversation. Why Dave's office? Dave would never hurt Alyssa. He loved her as much as I did, maybe more. I had always been a little envious of her delicate beauty and being an only child had to have been wonderful. I smiled, on the other hand, she always told me she loved my brash beauty and would give anything to have grown up in my boisterous family of eight. I headed back hoping to catch more of the conversation, but finally the door opened to the interrogation room. Dave had a look of fear in his eyes. I stood to go in the room as Senetti called me, and Dave grabbed my arm and nearly begged, "Don't go in without a lawyer."

I shrugged him off. "Dave I'm not a suspect. Let me get this over with…you, didn't do anything and neither did I."

Senetti came up. "Just give me a minute Senetti…please" Dave said as Senetti took a step back. "Ellen, for once, listen to me. I know what I'm talking about, innocence doesn't always matter."

I disregarded him… "I have to find my friend Dave. I have nothing to hide. On the other hand maybe you do. I am curious to know why they are getting a search warrant for you office." I pulled myself free and left him standing there as I walked in and sat down in a chair facing Senetti.

Senetti began "First, you are not a suspect, as you just told your husband. These questions are aimed at helping us understand more about you, your husband and your friends to shed any light on the situation. Ok?"

I nodded.

"Ok then." He hit the button on the recorder. "Let's start with the day Alyssa disappeared. You say you were supposed to meet her for lunch."

"Yes. We are both very busy, but always schedule lunch once a week, on Tuesdays so we can catch up and plan our next outing."

"So was this out of the norm for Alyssa to cancel?"

"It was out of the norm for her to cancel with me. Alyssa sticks to a schedule. She explained to my secretary that she had to miss and would call to explain later. It wasn't like her, but I knew she would have a good explanation if she had to cancel."

"Did meeting with your husband seem like a good explanation."

That question took me off guard...I hesitated "I didn't know she had met with my husband, and I guess yes, it does throw me a bit that she would cancel, she must have been worried about the malpractice suit."

"Had she mentioned the suit to you?"

"No."

"Would you say you were close?"

"Very"

"Do you find it strange she didn't mention anything about a problem with a client."

"All I can think is it must have just come up, because she would have told me."

Senetti pushed, "Even if she were meeting with your husband?"

He hit a cord and he knew it, because I was still wondering about the search warrant for his office. "Yes" I said. "and I don't like what you are implying Mr. Senetti."

"It's my job to ask Mrs. Martin" he came back "and what makes you think I'm implying anything?"

"I overheard your eager beaver Morris calling some woman named Linda to get a search warrant for my husband's office. What possible reason could you have for that?"

"I'm asking the questions Mrs. Martin." Senetti said. I knew I immediately disliked this man and the way he spoke to me.

"Yes you are Mr. Senetti, but if you want my cooperation, you might want to save the attitude for my husband; it won't work with me."

"So I've gathered." He said. "Let's go on. So, you never got the explanation, right?"

"The next call I got concerning Alyssa was from Dante asking if I knew where she was."

"How did he seem when he called?"

"He was frantic. He knew if she wasn't home and hadn't called something was wrong, as did I."

"So then what?"

"I tried her cell. I headed over to their house. I called every friend I could think of to try and find out where she might be…no luck."

"Ok then….let's go back to your personal relationship with the Morelli's." Senetti said.

"Alyssa and I were good friends in high school and became great friends in college. It was a once in a lifetime friendship…I have never had a friend like her. We were inseparable in college and she's still my best friend." I swiped at my eyes and my voice shook.

He changed the subject quickly, "Tell me about your day yesterday Mrs. Martin."

"Well briefly speaking it was a typical day. I had two surgeries early in the morning, and a couple of consultations. After Alyssa cancelled, I grabbed a sandwich to eat at my desk and dictated the consultations for my secretary to type up over my lunch hour. I had one surgery scheduled for the afternoon. I made the rounds to check up on my patients, stopped by my husband' office to leave some allergy medicine off with his secretary for him on the way home and spent the rest of the afternoon reading, catching up on my medical journals."

"Where did you do your reading?"

"I went home…took off my shoes….got a glass of wine and started reading. I was still reading and taking notes when Dante called."

"Ok, was Alyssa a friend with your husband as well as you?"

"Yes, very much so."

"So she could have been in the backseat of your husband's car?"

"What?"

"Well, as his friend or your friend maybe you all could have been in your husband's car?" He questioned.

I thought for a moment "No not really. It's a new car. I've never even been in the backseat, nor has anyone else that I know of. What makes you think Alyssa has rode in Dave's car?"

Senetti looked like the cat that swallowed the canary, "Well Mrs. Martin was definitely in the back seat of your husband's car. Her fingerprints were found there."

"What? How do you know?" I blurted out.

"Well it seems both you and your friend were arrested once for drugs and he smiled, I believe indecent exposure. Would you like to explain that?" He seemed to be enjoying this and I was getting even more irritated.

"Were you ever young Mr. Senetti or ever do anything stupid? I will admit we had our fun. We studied all the time, worked hard, and once in awhile needed to play harder. We experimented from time to time. And yes, once in awhile we smoked pot and or drank alcohol. It was a great stress reliever."

"And the indecent exposure" he questioned trying, and not succeeding, in hiding his smile.

And for the first time I had to smile as I remembered what we had done that night. "It had been a long week. We had classes all week and tested on Saturday, so by Saturday afternoon nearly every med. student could be found in the bar. We started drinking beer, then someone bought a few shots, one thing led to another and one of the guys told us he had some weed. So, about a half dozen of us went back to our room, lit the incense, turned down the lights and he lit the pipe. After a couple drags we were definitely buzzing. We were playing 'Truth and Dare' Alyssa had a dare to flash the nerds across in the adjoining dorm through the window. She wouldn't do it alone, so I did it with her. They could see us clearly through their window. They loved it. It was getting a little more risqué as we kept daring each other to go farther and farther, they showed something... we showed something; however, what we didn't see was the RA coming home and God knows she wasn't fond of any of us. She turned us in....end of story" I blushed.

I knew that wasn't the end of the story, but I certainly wasn't going to share that with Senetti. Even though my brain had been in a fog from the drugs and alcohol, my memory was not hazy. There had been five of us. Wayne, Todd, Halley, Alyssa, and I. By the time we started to play the game Todd had already passed-out on one of our beds. Wayne was the one who suggested we play 'Truth or Dare' and since he was the one who was always generous with his pot, I figured he was hoping for a kiss, and I figured I owed him that much. The whole thing took a turn I wasn't expecting.

One of the questions was "Have you ever made it with a woman?" No one had. Then it was "Would you ever kiss a woman?" Again, there were only three of us girls there and we all shook our heads negative. I knew where it was leading, when the first dare I got was to kiss Halley and then Alyssa. I remember thinking it was weird, but thought "what the hell, let him get his rocks off." Everything seemed more intense, magnified. I gave them each a quick peck.

"No way, you gotta' slip 'em some tongue," he said.

"You didn't say that" I argued. "You said kiss and I did."

Well obviously the next dare was a kiss that was timed, with tongue. It was Alyssa's dare and she kissed Halley first. It was weird watching them kiss, but not bad really, so when it was my turn she turned to me and I felt her wet, soft lips on mine. They were so different from male kisses, her tongue was so small and hot as it darted in my mouth. It didn't really repulse me; it was just different. The next dare we made Wayne undress in front of the window and when I told Senetti we flashed the guys across from our room, that was the truth. They didn't appreciate Wayne, but his next dare was for us to undress in front of the window. I actually enjoyed their enthusiasm as they whistled out the window. That's probably what alerted the RA to us in the first place. I think we were actually getting high from pushing the limits, because no one was taking a 'truth' it was all 'dares'. It was only a matter of time before we were dared to kiss naked, first it was Wayne, then each other. Halley dared Alyssa to put her hand on my breasts. She didn't just put it there, she fondled them gently. Then, I was dared to kiss Haley's breasts for one minute. I remember licking softly around them before I gently nipped them with my teeth and then began to suck them. She moaned and I think it surprised me, because I really hadn't thought about pleasing another woman before. Then, Alyssa put her hand between my thighs. I was wet. Her dare was to stroke me. She gently moved her fingers up and down. I never thought I would ever do this with another woman, but the pleasure was better than with the amateur males I had been with. She knew exactly where to touch me and when my next dare was to insert my finger inside of Haley I knew I left her aching for release. Then the game was forgotten, the guys watching were forgotten and we experimented like we never had before. I felt hands on my breasts and fingers inside of me; I felt a mouth on my clit. I didn't know whose hands or whose mouth and I didn't care as I nearly exploded then, but when Haley and Alyssa both centered their attention on my wetness with hands and mouths, I climaxed like I never had before. As I lay spent, I thought the blood was pounding in my head, but realized it was cops banging on the door. I slowly came out of my sex/drug intoxication to grab Wayne's shirt and put it on before the officers came through the door. They were fortunately middle age men and they saw us as daughters, and their biggest desire seemed to be to clothe and protect us. It went harder for the guys. The entire incident had been embarrassing, but I had put it down to youth and inexperience.

CHAPTER 8

Morelli – Meetings

*A*fter a sleepless night and throwing back too many scotches I looked and felt like hell. The whole damn thing seemed like a nightmare and the shrill ringing of the phone didn't help my already throbbing head.

"Hello" I barked into the phone.

"Dante, it's Dave I need to talk to you."

"I don't need a lawyer right now Dave, I need my wife. And I can't believe you of all people have the balls to fucking call me."

"That's what I need to talk to you about. I'm being set up Dante. You know I'm not stupid, so I'm begging you here."

"Fucking fine. You got an hour get over here."

"I would rather meet at Bocco's. You sound like you need some coffee anyway."

"Yeah that will work. It might do me some good to get out of here…be there in 15 minutes."

Sal, was sitting in the living room. Sal weighs 260 easy and towers above me at 6'4". His shaved head makes him look something like a bulldog. I walked toward him and threw him the keys to my car. I'm thinking I'm probably the only man he doesn't intimidate. There are no bounds to his loyalty. He doesn't think, he just does what I say. He is the muscle behind the brains in my outfit.

"Drive me over to Bocco's."

"Sure. I'll bring the car around." He seems relieved. Sal is more a man of action.

I splashed cold water on my face and put on a fresh white shirt. Walking out into the foggy morning air I wait only seconds before

Sal pulls around the driveway to pick me up. He is a man of few words and we ride in silence. "Wait for me." I say as I get out of the car. "This shouldn't take long." He nods in answer.

Dave is waiting at a table. He has a cup of espresso in front of him and has ordered mine as well. As I sit across from him, I think Dave looks worse than I feel. He looks apprehensive, jumpy and I see a real flash of fear as he looks at me. It almost saddens me to know I invoke fear in even my friends. "Ok Dave you called me. To save time I already know my wife's fingerprints were found in the backseat of your car. I also know they were on the outside where they found the blood."

He choked… "Ok Dante first we are all friends here and you know I would never go behind your back with your wife."

"Yeah, even if you wanted to, you wouldn't 'cuz you know I would kill without a seconds hesitation."

"I do know that, yes. That's why I know someone is setting me up. I have no idea how fingerprints could get in my car. I don't know where the blood or hair came from. I'm telling you I took that car to work and never left until I came to your house when I got Ellen's call. The car is new. Hell I didn't even think anyone had ever been in the backseat. Now they tell me they have prints, hair and blood. I don't know how the hell it could have happened. I would say it's fucking impossible, but obviously it isn't."

I watched him to see if he was telling me the truth. I believed him. "You know I do believe you. I have no idea who is doing this or why. I have to think it is someone after me and not my wife. But I will tell you Dave if I ever even suspect you lied to me or you ever touched my wife there is no rock in this entire fucking universe that I will leave unturned to find you. And not even God will be able to help you.

Again I saw the fear in his eyes. He knew I too was telling the truth. "This conversation is over. I think until this is all resolved it would be in both of our best interests not to have any further contact."

"I agree," he said. I could see relief sweep over him.

I turned and walked out to my waiting car to go back home when my cell phone rang. "Hello."

"This is Lt. Mike Senetti"

"I figured I would hear from you…I don't suppose your calling to tell me you've found my wife."

"No sorry…but I do need you to come to the station. There's a few points we need to go over again."

"If you just want me to reiterate what I already told you yesterday, you can come to my house." I hung up the phone without giving him a chance to answer. If I had to go through all this shit again I was going to do it on my terms, not in a dingy room with a hard, filthy table and cold uncomfortable folding chairs. Besides it gave me some kind of satisfaction to tell Senetti what to do. I didn't think many men could or would.

"Home Sal." I said and laid my head back on the seat and closed my eyes. What I wouldn't give to crawl in bed with Alyssa right now…hold her in my arms……

I dozed and I was holding her in my arms. I was back to that first date again. I remember standing at her door behind a dozen long stem roses. She came to the door in blue jeans and a t-shirt and behind the roses I had on a dress shirt, pants and tie. "Guess I should have asked where we were going I said?

"I thought we could grab a burger, beer and bowl," she giggled as she grabbed the flowers and stuck them in what I believe was an old mayonnaise jar. She then looked me over, undid my tie and pulled it over my head flinging on the couch. She untucked my shirt, undid a few buttons at my neck, stood back again and said "you'll do."

She made me smile and I gotta say her hands at my neck and at the waist of my pants nearly made me sweat. What the hell was it about this woman? I had bedded many and yet she made me nervous with only the slightest feel of her hands. "You wanna take my car" she started to say and quit in mid sentence, because there was the limo I had rented to take us out to supper. She looked a little flustered then we both started laughing and crawled in as the chauffer opened the door.

"If you want beer, we can go get some" I said, enjoying watching her squirm for a change as I held up a bottle of Arott.

"You remembered."

"Of course, I told you it's my favorite."

"Mine too and wine is just fine" she replied.

"Ok then, where are the best burgers in town?" I asked.

"Liberty Burgers." She said.

"Liberty Burgers it is" I told the driver. We had several glasses of wine as the driver worked his way through evening traffic. I didn't care how long it took to get there. I was enjoying the wine and the company. They weren't good burgers, they were possibly the best burger I had ever eaten or maybe it just seemed that way, just as good as the ones at Clown Alley back home. I even liked watching her eat. She loved food. She wasn't shy about eating like some women. She smiled, and talked and ate, in fact, she ate as much as me. I couldn't believe, as thin as she was, that she could put food away like that.

"Bowling now?" I asked.

"You know I picked this fancy restaurant, how bout you decide the entertainment?"

"Well we could bowl, but I was thinking a walk might be nice."

"Sounds wonderful I'm a little full."

"I should think so." I laughed.

She said, "Peanut butter and jelly was a long time ago for breakfast. I didn't have time for lunch and I do love burgers….thanks."

"Anytime." I was thinking if I had my way she would never have to have peanut butter and jelly again if she didn't want it. I told the driver to pick a nice place. He took us to the older section of Philadelphia so we could look at the historic homes. We walked for about forty-five minutes, the conversation never lacking, then once again she got the jump on me.

She stopped, grabbed my hand and asked, "are you going to kiss me?"

Caught off guard, I looked down at her and smiled "sure I am, but do you think maybe it could be my idea…not that I haven't been thinking about it." I loved her unabashed candor. I looked down at her, tipped her chin "guess I'm ready I said." I saw her grin before I lowered my lips to hers and I held her….held her in my arms. I reached for her hand to find her fingers crossed. I looked at her questioningly.

She looked embarrassed "I'm superstitious. I cross my fingers for good luck."

"Good luck?"

"Lucky that I met you, lucky you came to see me, hope I'm lucky enough you liked kissing me so that you'll come back. I had my fingers crossed the first night we met on my blind date and it worked so ....." She trailed off looking sheepish.

"Well then I'm doing it too, because it works. This is our sign.... and it is lucky. I loved seeing you again, I loved the burgers, the walk and most of all kissing you."

We crossed our fingers.... and I saw her cross them over and over in a hundred different places...I saw her cross them the last time I saw her when she drove away....

I jolted awake as Sal braked the car....fingers, oh baby to see you cross your fingers again...I turned to get out before Sal saw the tears leaking out beneath my sunglasses.

CHAPTER 9

Morelli – Questioning

$\mathcal{I}$ got out of the car and went in the house. It wouldn't do to show any weakness in front of Sal. Hell the man probably wouldn't cry if his own mother died. Maybe another scotch would dull the pain. I reached for the decanter and sloshed it in the glass. The doorbell rang. Sinetti I thought. Let him wait. I tossed back the drink and felt the liquid warm its way down my throat and burn into my empty stomach. I poured another for good measure and walked to the door, scotch in hand… "Come in Senetti." I was hoping the liquor took hold fast. I needed it to deal with Senetti right now.

"Little early for scotch." He observed.

"Little early for a social call." I shot back. "See you have your side kick. Want a drink?"

"Dante Morelli…Detective Morris from homicide and no I don't drink anymore, at least not for eleven years anyway." He said in way of introduction.

"Homicide?" My hand started to shake, the scotch spilling over the edge. "Why homicide? Have you found her?"

"No..I just wanted to be upfront about this. You know how many hours have gone by as well as I do. Morris here is a good man, gonna be a hell of a detective and I would like to think he can learn something from me and I can use his fresh perspective in this."

I relaxed my grip on the glass. "Ok Senetti, Morris, have a seat let's get on with this."

"We have checked your alibi, everything checks out. From what we understand you and your wife had a good relationship. However the question still remains why she didn't tell you about the malpractice suit. It seems strange that in a good marriage, one where you communicate she wouldn't tell you."

"I agree, I thought she told me everything. I was as surprised as anyone that she would go to Dave before discussing it with me. It must have happened that morning after she left."

"Why didn't she call you before she met Dave?" Senetti asked. His sidekick didn't miss a beat, he was taking notes on everything.

"She may have been afraid to tell me, because I would be very upset if anyone threatened her in anyway." I was thinking she knew I would kill anyone who even crossed her the wrong way and that was the only explanation that seemed plausible, but figured Senetti knew that. "She would have told me that evening, after all Dave was a friend."

Morris looked up at the word "was" and Senetti picked up on it "Was?" he asked with a nod to Morris

"You know as much as I do Senetti. Dave was the last one to see her, fuck I even hate that. I should have been with her; I should have seen her. It looks like there's some pertinent evidence, thanks to your little CSI team, pointing to Dave right now and I'm not saying it doesn't look just a little too convenient, but I would be hard put to call him a friend."

"How the hell do you know what evidence has been found? It hasn't been released yet." Morris stopped writing and asked. Senetti just shook his head and held his hand to quiet Morris. He knew I had my ways. I just smiled in answer. Morris might be good, but he had a lot to learn and the most important thing would always be, trust no one.

At that point Sal filled the doorframe. He silently made a nod in my direction. "Excuse me for a minute this might be important." I said knowing it was if Sal interrupted.

We retreated into the next room, "What is it Sal?"

"They found the car." Sal said hurridly.

"Where is it?" I shot back.

"Down at a chop shop at Hunter's Point." Sal answered in his abbreviated answers. If I didn't value the man, he would irritate the hell out of me. If he could speak in sentences instead of giving me his typical three word answers he would save us both a lot of time.

"So do they know who's it is and that we know where it is?" I asked.

"Nope"

"Bring the car, let's go." I said relieved that I could finally act on something. I walked back through the doorway. "I'm going to have to terminate this conversation. My guys have found her car."

"Ok. Then tell us where it is." Senetti replied looking resigned. Once again I had beat him at his own game.

"No. I don't think so."

"Then we will follow you." Senetti said. "You don't need any more trouble right now Morelli."

I couldn't argue that point. "You can ride with me then." I said. "After all it wasn't your choir boys that found it now was it? And it wouldn't work nearly as well for the cherries to be flashing to get the info. we need. It's my way now. You can come or stay here. The choice is yours."

"We're in." Senetti said. Morris closed his notebook and without a qualm followed Senetti. The kid was going to be good; he knew when he had to leave his code of ethics behind when there was something bigger at stake.

"Let's go through the house to the connected garage. We will take Sal's car the windows are tinted and hopefully with your car still in the driveway the media assholes will stay put."

Senetti agreed.

We left in silence the North Beach area towards Hunter's Point district with Sal's solid form behind the wheel. I could see Morris inquisitively looking at Senetti in the rearview mirror. Senetti gave him a nod as if to say, "You made the right choice kid. Things are gonna go down, but they are gonna be fine."

As we got closer Senetti asked me who owned the shithole. I relay the question to Sal.

"Oscar Zapedas" was Sal's quick retort.

"Why the fuck didn't you tell me that?" Senetti asked.

"I just found out myself and quite frankly I didn't give a shit who owned it." I said.

For the edification of Morris, Senetti said "Oscar Zapedas runs all the local chop shops in the bay area. He buys the stolen cars, chops 'em, then distributes them."

Morris said "Uh Senetti, I know what a chop shop is, explanation unnecessary."

I had to smile as I heard Senetti say "sorry, I'm sure you do."

"Hey Senetti maybe the kid can teach you a few things." I couldn't resist the dig.

Senetti grunted in reply. The conversation ended abruptly as we pulled up to the shop.

Sal was a man on a mission. He got out of the car and went in. He knew his job well. I didn't need to tell him to check to see if it was safe to enter the building. That's what Sal was all about. Sal came to the door and gave me a curt nod. "It's clear" I said "let's go." Senetti and Morris got out of the car and followed me in. I turned to Senetti and softly said "Welcome to my world."

Senetti nodded affirmatively, and though I didn't like him much, I admired him. The man had balls.

It was noisy as Sal ushered us into Zapedas office, but when the door closed behind and Sal stationed himself to guard the door the silence was deadly. Zapeda was behind his desk. He was a scrawny, greasy looking weasel of a man. He stood as I walked in the room and offered his hand. I could see the filth under his nails as I ignored his hand and left mine in my pockets. "I'm sure you know who I am." I said.

Zapedas nearly groveled as he whinned "Of course I know who you are Mr. Morelli. How can I be of service to you?"

"You have something that belongs to me" I said pointedly "and before you answer you better make sure you give me the right answer and by that I mean the fucking truth, which I'm sure is something you aren't used to." I warned. "And if you don't" I threatened "you will find your slimy ass smeared all over one of the trunks of your own fucking stolen cars." I finished matter of fact.

The man nearly stuttered. I could tell the sleazy little bastard was scared shitless, so much so that I knew he wasn't going to lie. "Sure, sure Mr. Morelli, anything, just tell me what you're looking for."

"It's a 1997 Mercedes SL 500 white. You have it here. Where did you get it? Where is it now?"

Zapedas, looked sick. He literally turned green. "The car came in late yesterday afternoon. And I gotta say it was a weird situation.

It was left in the middle of Market Street running and the keys were in it."

"And now…?"

It's in the shop getting stripped as we speak."

"Show me." Now I was the one who felt ill. Was my wife in the car when someone took it? Where was she now?

We walked through the garage. Cars were being dismantled at a startling rate, but all that mattered to me was the shell of the car I saw in the back corner. It was the shell of the car that was my wife's. As we walked to the car and looked inside I tried to see if I could find anything that told me if my wife had been hurt in that car. "Look it over" I told Senetti and Morris. "If you want to pull it down to headquarters for your team to look at I'm sure that can be arranged." I looked at Zapedas.

"Certainly" Zapeda said. Getting more and more nervous. "Just remember you weren't here," he added for the benefit of Senetti and Morris.

Senetti purposefully ignored him. I'm sure he would have liked to have ground him under his heel, but right now that wasn't important. Thankfully he was searching every inch of the car. I thought maybe he found something when he asked for a flashlight.

As Zapeda gave Senetti the flashlight, he handed me the keys.

Just when I doubted they would find anything, my wife's car was as immaculate as our home, her office and her life… Morris, who had taken over the flashlight pulled out something from under the passenger seat. It must have been put on the console and fell between it and the seat.

Now I am a man who shows no emotion, but I'm sure the shock showed on my face, and I felt my body go rigid when I saw the receipt to a motel room registered for two under my wife's name; A motel room where I had never stayed.

My head reeled. There is no way I can conceive that my wife would be disloyal. She would never have an affair? I know she loves me. There can't be anyone else. For a suspicious man, I never once suspected my wife of anything. I still didn't. There had to be an explanation. What the fuck was I going to do? I needed her here. I needed her to tell me she got the room for something or someone else. Fuck…..I just needed her.

As if Senetti could read my thoughts. He came up and said "You want us choir boys to look into this one?"

"I know there is nothing here. And when you find out more about my wife, you'll know it too, but yeah go ahead, check it out." I said shaken from the whole experience. "Let's get out of here."

We turned and walked out. I gave Sal a nod and he turned back around. "Be back," he said as we got in the car. He was back within minutes and I knew Zapeda wouldn't ever lie to anyone again.

"Home?" Sal asked.

"Yeah?" I answered.

Senetti's phone buzzed. "Senetti here. That was quick… nice to have a lab so close. Good. Go ahead…..Where? Hmm. Sorta puts a new spin on things. Thanks. We'll be there in about 30-45."

"So the DNA results are in?" I asked.

"Yes they are." Senetti answered.

"You going to tell me what they found or do I use my own sources. I will know as soon as you do, so you might as well tell me."

"Let me go back to the lab and confirm everything then I will come talk to you. Does that work for you?" Senetti asked.

I could actually hear compassion in his voice and it scared the hell out of me. I knew then the blood on that car was probably Alyssa's and he was trying to spare me and right now I didn't want to hear it. "That will work," I said knowing I was only prolonging the agony at this point.

I felt her keys in my pocket. I gripped them tightly. If only those keys could bring me something, some kind of hope that she wasn't dead. Surely she couldn't be. I felt I would know it if my wife was dead and I just didn't or couldn't believe that she was.

We pulled up to the house. Senetti said, "I'll be back." as they climbed into their car to leave, I nodded my thanks. Sal drove the car to the garage to put it away. I used Alyssa's keys that had never left my hands to unlock the door. I only wished it could be her hands unlocking the door, or better yet, she would be standing on the other side of the door when I opened it.

The house was empty. No one there on the other side. I threw the keys across the room as I reached for the bottle of scotch.

CHAPTER 10

Senetti – DNA

$\mathcal{A}$s we drove away from the Morelli home, questions were thrown at us from all directions. As I looked back through the throng of reporters, I saw a powerful man crushed and as evil as I thought Dante Morelli was, I sympathized with him.

As Morris is fingering the hotel receipt, he starts reading it. "Sunday, March 2 1997, 12:38" he mumbled. "Do you think she was cheating on him? This doesn't look good, but he seems almost positive she wouldn't? Yet wouldn't he know about this if she told him everything?"

Senetti said "Maybe she's a match for Morelli. Maybe his angel isn't the angel he thought she was. First things first, let's go find out what the DNA can tell us, then you can check out the hotel."

"Jesus" Morris said as we pushed our way through a barrage of reporters. "I thought we left all these fucks back at Morelli's. You know my idea of hell is being surrounded by reporters shoving their mics in my face and firing questions at me."

We walked past the garage to the CSI lab. Tom and Linda met us. Tom had the results in his hand. Not trusting anyone, I said, "Let's go in the conference room and shut the door."

After the door was closed Tom said, "You better sit down for this."

"Who else has seen these results?" I asked.

"We are the only ones who have seen it." Linda said.

"Let me start out by telling you once again, nothing leaves this room. Morelli has been finding out information before I do. We have someone leaking information somewhere, so if he finds out about this DNA from anyone, but me, I will know where to start looking."

They nodded solemnly, and Tom opened the folder. He handed the first page to me. It was the report on the testing of the blood. There was a rap at the door.

"Yeah" I said irritated at the interruption.

"Coffee" came the answer from the other side of the door.

"I had them get us some coffee." Linda explained. "All you been going on Senetti is coffee and adrenaline, so I thought I may as well feed the monster. Bring it in."

"Thanks" I said in a way of apology when I saw the coffee, sandwiches and cookies on the tray. I couldn't remember the last time I had eaten anything either.

The cop stood at the door. "Leave" Linda said abruptly. And only after he left and the door closed did Tom begin.

"Now if you are looking at the report it shows, the blood is definitely a match. It is Alyssa Morelli 99.9% chance of that. The blood showed traces of benzodiazephine, specifically diazepam."

I raised my eyebrows questioningly.

"Valium" Linda supplied. "We must assume that she was drugged and placed in the car."

Tom glanced at me briefly as if I weren't very bright and continued, "On the second report, on the hair follicle, it too is a definite match to the strands we found from the brush in Allyssa's home; however, the hairs taken from the brush do not show the trauma that the ones taken from the vehicle showed. This seems to indicate that her hair was pulled going in or out of the car."

"Unless he pulled her hair during some hot, rough sex in the back seat of the car." Linda added.

Morris raised his eyes and looked at her as though he was seeing her for the first time. Tom moved on, though all business, "As much as I appreciate your train of thought, we found no semen or vaginal fluid in the car." Morris slouched back down and I suppressed a grin.

However, speaking of sex and vaginal fluid, take a look at this next report. When the sweep was done of the Martin home, vaginal fluid was indeed found in the Martin's bed, and it was Alyssa Morelli's.

"Holy shit" Morris said.

"Fuck" I said.

"Guess that answers my question as to her cheating on the hubby" Morris said.

"Fuck, fuck, fuck, Dave Martin is a dead man. This does not leave this fucking room." I said.

Tom went on as if Morris and I hadn't said anything "also in the bed was more of the same hair follicle matches."

"That nails it!" Linda said. "no pun intended, but it's definitely sex!"

And even through the seriousness of the situation Morris had a spark in his eyes and a smile tugging at the corner of his lips "gotta appreciate her one track mind" he mused.

The implications were staggering. I walked to the board and wrote three names: Dave Martin, Dante Morelli, Ellen Martin. Under Dave Martin's name I wrote. Affair. We started throwing out ideas.

Linda said, "Well, maybe she had an affair with Martin and tried to break it off. He was obsessed with her and if he couldn't have her no one would."

I answered "Why would he do that? He had a wife just as beautiful and successful?"

Morris added "Why have an affair with a woman whose husband would defiantly kill you without thinking twice?"

Tom being the practical one said, "Well the evidence points to Dave Martin."

"But the evidence seems too contrived. Dave is a smart man; he knows better than to cross Dante Morelli." I said.

Linda threw in "passion knows no bounds....I have yet to meet a man who thinks with his head when something else is doing the thinking for him."

Morris mused "there she goes again."

"I just hope your wrong, for Martin's sake I hope your wrong. Anything else on Dave Martin? No, then let's look at Ellen Martin. Up to this time we haven't considered her, but a woman's scorn knows no bounds you know. She may have discovered the affair." I said.

They all started talking at once. "Hold on. Who thinks there is a possibility that Ellen killed her best friend out of jealousy?" Neither man thought Ellen did it. Linda, however did.

"Ok Tom, give me your view."

"All the evidence points to Dave Martin. It was his car; he has the hour that he says he was with Alyssa, but where? No one can verify they were in his office the entire hour. His wife, while beautiful, is overbearing. I might have an affair if I were married to her."

"Hm maybe he shoulda just killed his own wife" I said trying for a bit of humor and remembering the attitude I had experienced with Ellen Martin in the interrogation room.

Tom came back, "but if Ellen did it she did a hell of a job framing her husband, would she want revenge that bad?"

Morris gave his two bits, "From what I saw, I think Ellen was sincerely worried about her best friend. She talked her husband into going into the precinct to answer our questions when he would have waited for a lawyer, because she wanted to find her friend as soon as possible."

Linda wrapped it up by saying "She wouldn't be the first woman to want to kill someone for cheating with her husband. You aren't thinking like a female here guys. Males fight something out and then you get over it. A woman holds a grudge. If Alyssa betrayed Ellen with Dave, then yeah, I think she would be angry enough and jealous enough to be the one to kill her. I know many women who would never actually kill, but I guarantee you they wanted to."

"This brings us to Morelli" I said. "You said men wouldn't want revenge. This man lives on it. He doesn't need to hold a grudge. He just erases it. It doesn't exist. For him it isn't jealousy or love, because I have no doubt he loved his wife. But he would kill her if she betrayed him. You don't betray Dante Morelli."

They all mumbled in agreement.

"Well, though we can't prove anything at this point I think you have all brought up some very valid points and possibilities here. What we have to do now is call a press conference for tomorrow morning. This will have to be moved from a missing persons case to a probable homicide. And I stress probable, since there is still no body. I need to let Morelli know before we disclose it to the media. Go home, get some rest and we will take a fresh look at this in the morning. Speak about it to no one." I warned them once again. "Lives are at stake here."

I wondered if I would get any sleep knowing my job wasn't complete. I walked up to my office and started to rifle through the reports, my head started spinning. I finally got up and turned off the light over my desk, time for some sleep Senetti I told myself.

I left the quiet building. It seems I'm always the last one to leave. I walked in the damp evening air with every intention of going home; however, I found myself driving back to Morelli's. After pulling up to his gate, I dialed his number.

"Hello" he said anxiously. I could tell he had been drinking, and it wasn't my voice he was hoping to hear.

"This is Senetti. I'm right outside. I've got some information for you."

"Come on in."

"You been drinking man and that's not a question." I said as I entered.

"Got a better idea?" He slurred.

"I just figured I owed you the DNA report from the blood on Dave's car. It's a match; it's Alyssa's blood. As of tomorrow morning the status of the case will be announced to the media as homicide. I'm sorry."

I never thought I would see Dante Morelli broken. "I kept thinking I would know if she were dead. I would feel it somehow. I don't fucking feel it." He said turning his back to me.

"Again sorry, thought you had the right to know before anyone else. I'll let myself out."

"I appreciate that." He said his voice catching on what I know was a sob. "Wait" he turned around "Between the two of us do you think Dave did it?"

"Well I wouldn't have thought so, and I still have a hard time believing it, but I'm gonna ask you to let us do our job, our way from here. Please." I added.

"I've seen how you do your job. And so far I have to say I'm not impressed."

"Well he was your friend; ask yourself if he would do that to you? Would Alyssa? Would she do that to her best friend? Everyone is a suspect right now, you included." I said.

He fired up "You know goddamn well I didn't kill my wife."

"I'm convinced of that, yes. But if I were to ask just about anybody else they would point the finger at you long before Dave. Goodnight Mr. Morelli. Call me if you need me." I picked up the keys to Alyssa's car Morelli had received that afternoon, which were laying on the floor and laid my card on top of them. As I turned to close the door softly behind me I saw Morelli looking at the pictures of his wife on the mantle.

CHAPTER 11

Morelli-Consequences

$\mathscr{I}$ looked at the photos on the mantle. Alyssa had them in some kind of order of events, no haphazard placement of pictures… all organized. The first picture I picked up showed Alyssa in a classy dress and me in my blue jeans carrying her in a chair. It took me back to the time I helped her move from her residency. We had continued a long distance relationship for six months. I flew to her or she flew to me about every other weekend and being with her every other weekend just wasn't enough; however, I knew her first choice of residency was in Nebraska and her second was San Francisco. She was offered either and I didn't know which she chose, but promised to move her wherever she wanted to go. I had showed up to move her in my t-shirt and blue jeans and she met me dressed up at the door with her fingers crossed and asked "Well Mr. Morelli I didn't know we were going bowling? That's in Nebraska. I think we are headed to San Francisco, am I dressed appropriately?" It was her way of telling me that though she had a chance to locate in Nebraska at the University of Omaha Med. Center or her second pick the San Francisco State University Medical Center, she passed up her first choice in Nebraska, because I was in San Francisco. "See these crossed fingers" she said "I think I'm gonna get lucky in San Francisco," she giggled giving me, and then Sal, a hug and a kiss"

"I've been crossing mine all along for your second choice" I said. "And honey you can bet your gonna get lucky in San Francisco. Have a seat lady." She sat in one of her kitchen chairs and I picked her up chair and all singing 'I Found My Heart in San Francisco' as

Sal snapped a shot blushing the entire time from her kiss. I had made up my mind to make sure she never regretted the choice.

The next picture I picked up was Alyssa and her dad on our wedding day. She adored her dad, he was probably the main man in her life, until she married me. After her mother's suicide, he was mom and dad for her. He was her everything. I had even offered for her and her dad to move in with us when we got married, but he was his own man and a proud man and would have none of it, even though he was very ill. Needless to say, Alyssa was devastated when he died two years after our wedding.

Then I looked at my family picture from the wedding. Like a typical Italian family there were at least twenty of us in the picture; however, I hadn't been as close to a single one of them as Alyssa had been to her dad. And since the death of our baby, I had disowned them. They were dead to me.

"The death of our baby," I mused as I moved to the picture of Alyssa, Ellen, Dave and I in the hospital room. That picture still made my heartache and now more than ever. It had been devastating when doctors couldn't find the heartbeat and induced labor and Alyssa gave birth to our stillborn baby. I lost my only son and Alyssa found she couldn't have more children. We managed to get through it, because we still had each other. And I don't think even then we could have managed, but our friends Dave and Ellen helped us through that terrible time and I could see how much they loved and supported us even in the picture. When Alyssa cried, Ellen cried. When I needed to be strong for Alyssa I could be weak with them, they were our shoulder, our rock.

It seems Dave and Ellen had been with us from the beginning. Ellen and Alyssa had been best friends from high school, through college, and they even moved to San Francisco with us. That had been an adventure in itself. I showed up with one of my dad's company trucks for Alyssa's stuff and Ellen and Dave were both struggling with college loans and were going to sell their belongings to get to California, and then live on whatever they had until they got some more stuff. When I found that out, I told them there was room on the truck and I bought Sal a plane ticket and told him to fly back home, that we would bring the truck. We had a trip home I will never forget and forged a friendship I had believed would last forever. We took turns driving. Dave and Ellen would take a turn driving while we slept and played in the back of the truck. Then we would drive while they slept. The girls might take a couple hours or the guys. We partied, we saw the sights, and we danced and sang. I can never remember a time I was more carefree and happy. I had love and friendship.

CHAPTER 12

Morelli - Morelli's Revenge

*A*s suspicious as I am, I never once suspected my friend would betray me. However, with the latest information from my very reliable snitch that my wife's vaginal fluid had been found in Dave's bed, I now questioned everything I once believed. What the hell was he thinking? He knew Alyssa was my life. The thought of him being with her was too much for me to bear. My heart had always been cautious and for the first time in my life, it had felt safe with her. Even if I couldn't trust Dave I had been sure I could trust Alyssa. I couldn't believe she would do this to me. For the moment, I buried the hurt with anger. I was consumed by a bloody rage that nearly devoured me. A wrong had been made and I was about to make it right. She deserved whatever happened to her and so did he. I was now a man totally controlled with deadly emotions. I needed to lash out; to make someone hurt as badly as I hurt. I knew that what I was about to do would render everything I valued and stood for useless; all because of the love of a woman and I was beyond caring. So, I made the call.....

"It's me we need to meet." I said, with every confidence that he knew who he was talking to.

"Yes I know," the voice on the phone replied.

"Pick him up. Call me when it's safe. Get the Doc" I said.

"Right you'll hear from me soon" the voice replied.

"Ok, just us." I replied.

I shook my head trying to clear the haze of hate. I marveled that a woman could bring me to this. I was going against every principle I had. This man had violated my life; for that he would pay with his.

It was only a matter of hours before the call came. "It's all good man."

As the garage doors opened for my car to come in one of my men looked in to make sure it was me. "Sir." Then he nodded for the gates to open.

As I got out of the car, I was met by brothers, not biological, but closer than blood ties. These men walking toward me had a loyalty that would never be in question. They had killed for me and would again. Brent, Sal, Nick and Drew walked up, each giving my hand a hard shake and hugging me in their huge arms. Sal asked if I was sure that this was what I wanted to do. I took a deep breath, but didn't hesitate. "Yes." Brent then gestured me into the house and Drew opened a door into what could have been a bedroom. However, there were only a couple of chairs and a table with various tools on it occupying the room. Dave was strapped to one of the chairs in the middle of the room with duct tape. He couldn't move or talk.

As I walked toward him my emotions almost got the better of me. This was once a man I trusted with my darkest secrets, my lies, aspirations, dreams and most of all the truth of the man I was. He knew even more than the men outside the door that Alyssa was the life I always wanted and yet he took that away. So he was here to talk or die.

As I pulled up a chair to sit next to him, I cursed myself for the tears sliding down my face. This was a man that I trusted and believed in for so long. I turned to look at him and through the tears he could see the hatred I felt and remorse for what I was about to do to him.

"Hi Dave" I said softly my voice catching. "I am going to take the tape off your mouth and I don't want you to say anything except what I ask you. Do you hear me? Nod yes or no."

As Dave nodded yes, his tears too streamed down his face. As I studied his face, I read sadness, confusion and a deep-seated fear.

I began to take the thick duct tape off his mouth.

I went to the door and opened it. "Everybody stay on this side of the door unless I tell you differently, except you Doc I'm going to need you." He sidled into the room. The others sat down waiting. I closed the door softly and turned to Dave.

"Hey Dave" I merely whispered.

"Hey Dante" he said as a sob caught in his throat.

"You know why you're here."

"I swear Dante I don't." He said it sincerely and if I hadn't been blinded by hatred and revenge I could have believed him.

"Please don't make me do this Dave." I whispered as I quickly turned away so he couldn't see my tears.

"D I love ya man I would never."

"Dave don't LIE TO ME." I screamed as I walked over to the table and Doc handed me a ball ping hammer without a word.

"I can't walk away from here Dave and neither can you, so don't, please don't even for a minute think you can talk your way out of this one. Why the fuck Alyssa? You more than anyone knew what she meant to me." My heart was fighting with what I was about to do. "I am only going to ask once. Where is she, what happened?"

As I received a look of confusion from Dave and no response the anger took over.

I pulled the hammer back and aimed at the point right to the middle of his kneecap. I swung and heard the pop of his knee shattering and felt it give.

Blood trickled down his chin as he bit his lip to try and silence his screaming as wave upon wave of pain crashed through his body. Yet as his eyes begged for mercy nothing came out of his mouth but the words "I didn't. I didn't." I pulled back and hit the other knee as his piercing shrieks made the stoic Doc cringe. It must have been more than the foursome outside the outer room could handle, because the door cracked open and a hesitant voice asked, "Is everything ok D?"

I turned to them "Close the fucking door now," I screamed like a man possessed, as the door closed without hesitation.

"Ok Dave" I coaxed as his tears mixed with the blood running down his trembling lips. His pain was mirrored in his eyes. "I need to know what you did with Alyssa. She was all I ever had. She was my life Dave. Save yourself if you can. I will give you your life for mine, but I need to know what happened to her. I swear I will hand you my gun and tell the boys to let you walk."

He watched as I opened the door and called the guys into the room. I explained that if Dave told us what happened to Alyssa he was a free man. And everyone there knew I was a man of my word. They nodded and stood back as I closed the door.

"Dante I didn't kill her and I didn't fuck her, but I wished I had so she would have never met a cold hearted fuck like you. You deserve to be lonely. How could you ever think that Alyssa or I would betray you? And if you think for one minute that I believe you are going to let me go free from here, then you must think I am one dumb son of a bitch. I will see you in hell." He spit out as he turned his head away resignedly.

"Oh no, you got it wrong Dave. You are going to wish you were in hell after I finish with you." I pulled back again. He knew what happened to Alyssa and I planned to fuck him up but good. I hit every joint one at I time smashing the bones underneath. The pain had gotten the best of him and his screams turned to silence as he passed out.

I hated the fact that he was unconscious. I had only begun to inflict his pain and he would never hurt like I did. I motioned for Doc to bring the bastard back to consciousness.

As the silence ensued the men came in. Nick and Sal looked at the battered man tied to the chair. Nick shook his head. "Jesus Christ Dante don't you think he would have talked if he knew where she was. No man holds out as he is being crippled. Are you sure, are you absolutely sure he deserved this."

I glared at him, but for once doubt entered my mind. Could I have made a mistake? Was I killing Dave because he slept with Alyssa? Or was I killing him because I believe he killed her? It didn't even matter anymore. One was as bad as the other. Alyssa wasn't coming back either way.

Doc worked on him to bring him to. A low guttural moan escaped from his lips. His eyes rolled back in his head, but he was lucid once again. I couldn't stand the moaning. It was worse than the screams. There was still something human in me connecting to this man. I told Sal to put the tape back on his mouth. He looked at me doubtfully. "Dante are you sure?"

"I said put the tape over his mouth." I gestured them out once again. They left reluctantly. I reached over to the table and grabbed the aluminum bat. His eyes watched me, but he didn't even offer resistance. He was resigned to whatever torture I inflicted on him. I lifted the bat over my head and managed to crash it down on both forearms. The bones could be seen in splinters through his arms like splinters of glass. He began to bleed profusely. His eyes closed and his body jerked, his head rolled back as he tensed to scream out, but not a sound escaped from behind the tape. He long ago had pissed his pants and the urine mixed with blood was rank. He was gagging behind the tape and was at risk of choking on his vomit. I turned my back and walked out the door, leaving him gagging and bleeding. I gestured to Doc "Keep him going. I don't care what you do, but I'm not done. Don't let him die yet."

Doc walked in, and as hardened as he was, he began resisting. "He's had enough. Just finish it Dante."

I placed the end of the cold metal, bloody bat on his cheek and said "He dies, you die."

"Your choice Dante." he said unflinchingly and met my eyes with a steely stare.

That was the pivotal point. I had crossed all that was dear to me and betrayed all that made me the man I am.

I broke eye contact with Doc and hung my head. "I need everyone to leave now." I said quietly.

Sal looked at me with despair; he knew I was going to commit the ultimate sacrifice. This was a friend and a brother. But who the fuck was I kidding, I couldn't let him live. I closed the door one more time as everyone left the room. My anger for this man was slowly dissipating. Death was a merciful act.

I walked to the table and picked up a fisherman's filet knife. Dave was near death already, but I still hung to the hope that he would at least tell me something if he were able.

It never happened. My work with the knife was swift and deft. Dave died shortly thereafter as the blood pooled at my feet. As I looked at the pulpy, broken mass before me, guilt washed over me. What had I done to my friend? Did he deserve it? I had my doubts. Dave had never been a strong man. He would have talked had there been something to say. I wondered now if he had ever been with Alyssa or if he would have had the balls to kill her. I walked to the door, opened it softly and nodded. Nick and Sal silently took the body and laid it on a plastic sheet rolled it up and carried him out. They placed him carefully in the trunk of Sal's car. I took no satisfaction in what I had done and what was the use, nothing had come from it. I wasn't any closer to what had happened to my wife, and the feeling I had hoped for by avenging her death completely eluded me.

As I hugged everyone before my departure, I couldn't help but see some kind of disappointment in their eyes.

CHAPTER 13

Senetti - Proof

*T*he phone ringing was like the jangling of my nerves. I couldn't stand its shrill cry, so I answered it by the second ring. "Hello."

The voice was a deep voice I recognized immediately "Senetti this is Morris from homicide."

"I know who it is, but shit Morris it's 4:30 in the morning. This better be good." I croaked out groggily.

"Oh it's good alright. Guess who I am starring at with his throat cut?" Morris said

As my adrenaline kicked in to hear what Morris had to say, sleep was no longer an issue.

I was alert now. "Who?" I asked fearful of the answer.

"Sal, Dante's boy. And by the looks of it there might be another body in the trunk. But we won't know 'till we get the car back to the shop." Morris replied.

"Holy shit Morris where? When?"

"We are towing the car to the garage now. The team is waiting there for us." Morris said. "Meet you there."

"I am getting dressed as we speak see you at the shop."

"Sounds good, see you there." Morris said.

As my heart raced from the information I had just received I couldn't help but think that I was getting closer to the people responsible for the disappearance of Alyssa Morelli. And it was a good deal, because I was in a race with Dante and getting nowhere fast. Everyone knew that if Dante ever found out who had anything to do with Alyssa's disappearance they would pray the law found them first. His anger was getting the better of him and at this point there was no one safe. Finally, I might have a much-needed break.

As I started to think of all that had transpired in the last week, I couldn't help but feel some sort of sadness for this man that I had come to hate. I put myself in his place for a moment and felt sadness that his love for his wife was something that could break a man, even a man like Dante Morelli. I seriously thought Dante had killed his wife in a jealous rage for having an affair with Dave, because nothing led me to any other conclusion. Could he have had Sal killed for knowing too much? Or was Sal there when Dante killed Alyssa? My mind was racing as fast as the car I was driving to the garage. I knew with Dante, it was only a matter of time before his anger overtook his better judgment and this might be it.

As I drove up to 850 Bryant, the main station, I could see news vans lined up waiting. As always the vultures wanted to see what they could get for the early morning news. The news of Sal's death would hit the streets and hit hard. New food for the birds of prey; God I hated the media. As I pulled into the gated garage, Morris was sitting near the entrance with the anticipation of my arrival.

"Bring me up to date Morris." I said swiftly getting out of the car.

"Well there are two bodies in the car. One of them is Sal's in the front seat of the car with his throat slit and the other is your suspect's attorney from what we can gather. Man they put a beating into this man like I have never seen. His body looks like ground beef." Morris replied shaking his head.

At this point my heart dropped. I looked at Morris with astonishment, "No fucking way Morris. Man this doesn't bend the rules; it changes the whole fucking game. We can't let anyone know about Dave's body until we figure out what the hell happened here. This has to stay quiet. I am assuming Dave was to be buried. Dante would never have let this happen if he thought someone else was with his wife. He is convinced it was Dave. Dante has to be behind this, but someone or something has just altered his plans. Morris, something is going to come to light now."

Morris was a little slow to follow "Well whatever happened here it's a mess. So you think he had Dave killed? But if that's the case, why Sal? He was closer than a brother to Sal. They were family. But then Dave and Dante were close too. I don't follow Senetti."

"Well I don't have a grasp on it all yet, but I'm starting to get somewhere." I said as we were walking down the hallways of the precinct toward the morgue. My hunches were coming to light. There was no doubt in my mind that Dante had everything to do with this, but I had to get the proof.

As I walked into the morgue, I couldn't help but turn my head in repulsion from the shock of the brutally beaten body. Looking at Dave's body angered me even more. This was a hate killing. I have been around long enough to know that whoever did this was pretty pissed. And again that only led me to one person.

It was pretty obvious that we had to find Dante and quick. As I was putting some thoughts together, my phone started to ring. I noticed that it was dispatch.

"Senetti here."

"Hi Mike this is dispatch. Sorry for calling you so early, but we had a guy call in regards to the disappearance of Alyssa Morelli. He asked to talk to the lead detective on the case. He said he would call back when he could be patched in. Will it be ok for me to pass him through when he calls? He wouldn't give me any other information."

"Why wasn't he patched in immediately?" I demanded.

"I tried three times and they all went to voice mail. Either you were on the phone or your service was not available." Dispatch replied.

"Thank you for the update, please call me no matter what. I can use anything at this point. I will be waiting here at the precinct if anyone calls, thank you." I said.

Damn I hate that I didn't get this mysterious call. Any kind of a lead at this point would be helpful. I sat down to collect my thoughts before I had to make that dreadful call to Dave Martin's widow. I always hate the look of shock, disbelief and finally grief, after I inform someone of the death of a loved one. Unfortunately, I have seen it far too often.

As I walked back in to the morgue after my phone call with dispatch I saw that Linda from CSI was already on the job.

"Hi Linda." I said.

"Hey Senetti, how are you on this fine morning?" she quipped, sarcasm dripping from her voice.

"Well, I am better than these two that's for sure" I said as I looked at the two bodies in front of me.

"Hey Senetti isn't this the guy we took DNA from the night that Morelli's wife went missing?" Linda said.

"Yep that's the poor bastard." I replied

"And prince charming here with the jugular sliced, wasn't he there too?" She said.

"Yeah, this isn't looking good for anyone that has anything to do with Dante Morelli. What are you looking at there Linda?" I asked.

"I was looking at this cut on Sal's neck. It was done with precision." She said.

"What do you mean?"

"You see how the slice is about three inches long facing downward. Whoever did this was a pro. He knew how and where to use a scalpel. This is a clean cut. This guy never had a chance. The other one was horrific, both legs shattered, his arms crushed, and finally if you look right under his armpit a slight wound that more than likely penetrated his heart, a merciful stab that finally brought death after his torture. These are two different murders, so you know what that means. We aren't talking about one killer, but two. This one," she said pointing to Dave, "had to have been killed first, because of the wounds to his body. Whoever did this took his time doing it. This story is different," she said moving to Sal. "From the amount of blood found in the car, he bled out pretty fast, in fact quick enough that he never had a chance to undo his seat belt. If you notice the amount of blood under his armpits, he tried to stop the bleeding, but probably passed out within minutes, fairly painless compared to his friend here," she explained.

"But why kill someone knowing there is a body in the trunk of that person's car?" I questioned, thinking aloud. "This doesn't make sense. I know Dave's murder was a revenge killing. And I was sure who was behind it. Dante was getting sloppy and it was more like minutes than hours before he screwed up. But Sal's death, why him? Did he see or do something? I couldn't imagine Dante having anything to do with Sal's death. How did it all connect?

"Well thank you Linda for your insight. Let me know if you find anything else, prints, DNA, blood, anything. Call me no matter what. And between you and I, let's keep what you just told me between us. I don't want anyone on the streets to know that Sal is dead yet. I have a few hours to get things moving before Dante starts to clean up his mess. And I hate to say it, but we might have rats here to tip Dante off." I cautioned.

"No sweat Senetti. I will be in touch as soon as I get it to the lab." Linda replied.

"Thanks. I knew I could count on you." I said over my shoulder as I left the morgue.

"Senetti hold up" Morris yelled as I was walking down the hallway away from the morgue.

"What's up Morris?" I asked as I stood in the middle of a cold hallway in between buildings.

"You know that phone call you were waiting for, from that mystery caller. It came again." Morris said.

"What! I told dispatch to fucking call me on my cell when that call came in."

"Calm down Senetti," he said "dispatch tried, but the cell service in here sucks to all hell. The guy is on hold. Just get to a phone so she can transfer that call. You better hurry 'cuz there's no telling on how long he'll stay on the line." Morris said.

As we ran from the one building to another and found a phone in an isolated spot where we could have a call transferred with no one hearing, I grabbed the phone and dialed in as soon as the connection was made. I breathlessly said "Dispatch this is Senetti can you transfer the call for me to this extension?"

"Sure is that ext. 2344?"

"Yes" I said with anticipation.

"Hello,,,,, Hello,,,,,,,," I said.

"Is this Mike Senetti" the strange voice on the other line asked?

"Yes, who is this? And what do you have for me?" I impatiently asked.

"Listen I am only going to say this once. So, pay attention. You have two bodies in the morgue right now and you are probably wondering what, where and when." he said echoing my thoughts.

"And how would you know that, if you don't mind me asking?" I countered.

"Because I was the last one with both of them so, no questions just shut up and listen." He sounded aggravated and I didn't want to risk losing him, so I bit back the urge to hit him with a barrage of questions and waited.

"Sorry, go ahead." I finally conceded.

"You are going to help me and I am going to help you. First, you are going to start off by hearing my side of the story. After that there will be no questions, not until I can be guaranteed that what I have to say will grant me full immunity. So, your job will be to go to the district attorney and get me immunity. Is that agreed?" The man sounded slightly desperate.

"So what do you have that makes you think you deserve full immunity? And better yet, what did you do that makes you need it?" I asked. "I'll need to hear a little information before I can guarantee anything. I am a fair man and if you give me what I need I will repay you in kind."

"I know the reason you have two bodies in that morgue" the man began again quietly.

"And how is that?"

"Because, I killed the driver. I had no choice. I overheard someone, who is very powerful, give the order for my death. And I think you know who killed the other person" the man said even quieter.

"I am going to need more than that." I said angrily.

"I have many options, one, I can disappear, and leave you with two unsolved murders, or you can get me the immunity that I am asking for and solve them both. Either way you need my help as much as I need yours." He came back logically.

"How do I know what you have is real? Your word against another will not hold up in court. So tell me what else you have to make me want to help you." I wanted badly to believe him, but it could be any asshole out there trying to pull my chain.

"Fine try this, the body in the trunk was going to disappear, in route to disposal; the materials used in the beating as well. Too bad they never made it. You have the body and I have the materials: a bat, hammer, and knife, all in a nicely sealed plastic bag. They have the murderer's prints and DNA on them. So, you have 'till this afternoon before I run, because after that Dante will know what transpired. I will have no choice, but to go into hiding. That's it. I will call you at noon, 'till then" the man said with a click.

"Wait ……Wait …." I said as I heard the phone disconnect. I had no doubt this man was telling the truth. He was exactly who I needed. But, I also realized the man was very bright and I couldn't dupe him, nor did he deserve it after coming forward. I had to work quickly if I was going to secure immunity for this man. The clock was now ticking and things where really starting to heat up.

Morris stood anxiously beside me, able to hear most of the conversation. "Want me to try to trace that call" he asked. Even though I knew nothing would come of it, I told him to give it a shot. Things were spinning out of control; nothing was ever going to be the same from here on. Someone saw Morelli actually kill Dave Martin and knowing this, it was only a matter of time before this person went in to hiding on his own, or disappeared by Morelli's hands. Either way I had little time to secure this witness if I didn't get immunity a.s.a.p.

Chapter 14

Senetti - News of Death

I started upstairs, phone in hand, dialing a friend that I had worked with in the District Attorney's office. I knew it was only going to be a short matter of time before Dante got word of either Sal's death, or the fact that Dave's body hadn't been disposed of, but was laying on a slab right next to Sal's in the morgue.

I dialed my friend Mark Macenna. He was a deputy District Attorney for San Francisco County. I knew he was someone I could trust to keep things quiet. Also, he could steer me in the right direction as to how I could get immunity for killing someone and mark it up to self defense in order to get the information and evidence I needed. I was worried that this was getting a little over my head, but I knew that I couldn't turn a blind eye to all these killings, nor was there any turning back now. My hate for what Dante could do and the power he wielded was stronger than my compassion for him for the loss of his wife. I was apprehensive that I would cross some lines that I shouldn't to get the information I needed and it concerned me that I wasn't troubled by it.

As I stumbled through my contact list on my cell phone looking for Mark's number I walked right by Brian Deecon. He was Dante's friend and some people in the department thought less of him because of it. I had believed myself more professional than that, but was having second thoughts.

"Hey Senetti, what's going on? I just heard they found Sal's body in his car a little outside the Sunset District." Brian commented.

"Yeah they found him with his throat cut in the front seat of his car." I replied trying hard not to mention that Dave was also in the car

"Shit D is really going to have a heart attack. You know we all grew up together." Brian said.

"No I didn't know that." I said as I was trying to walk away.

"Well, I see that you have to run. I am going to the morgue and check out what the hell happened." Brian said

Shit, I thought I could keep this quiet, but I couldn't trust anyone in this department to keep their mouth shut.

"Well before you go, I think I should tell you something else. I need you to keep that under your hat for a few hours." I said.

"What's that Mike?" Brian asked.

"Well the truth of it is, that when you go to the morgue you are going to find more than one body with the CSI team. What we have here is a double, two bodies, two different styles." I said regretfully.

"Will you quit talking all this secretive bullshit and just tell me what you mean?" Brain spit out.

"Well there are two bodies. Sal's was found in the front seat with his throat slit and the other is Dave Martin who you know was my suspect in the Morelli disappearance. Now I need you to do me a favor and keep this quiet. I know you and Morelli are friends. But I need to get a handle on what the fuck is going on here. This is going to get messy for everyone involved if we don't get it under control. You hear me." I said emphatically.

"Clearly I hear you, but why hide this from me. I have never given Dante shit when it comes to me doing my job. I told you that the night Alyssa was reported missing, I resent you implying I'm a rat." Brian said as he stormed off.

As I watched Brain leave, I had more pressing issues. I had no time to waste on him or anything else. So, I dialed Mark's number with the hope he would pick up.

"Hello this is Mark Macenne." he said.

"Hi Mark, don't know if you remember me, but this is Mike Senetti from missing persons." I said.

"Yeah, I remember. We had a couple of cases together." He said.

"You know that I have been investigating the disappearance of Alyssa Morelli. I have a suspect that I have been working on. I think he had something to do with a couple of murders that happened last night that I believe are connected." I said.

"Slow down Senetti. Everyone knows that you think Morelli killed his wife, but you don't have any proof." Mark said.

"Well let me finish. Proving he killed Alyssa will come in time, but I'm almost positive he killed her lover. I have a witness who is in possession of the physical evidence. He has the weapon that killed Alyssa's lover and he swears that it all leads back to Dante Morelli. Now, I only have a small window of time here, but I need immunity for him. He has admitted to killing one of Dante's right hand men, in self defense, because he overheard a conversation that he was going to be killed, so basically he beat Dante's man to the punch by slitting his throat, so it could conceivably be ruled self defense. Apparently, he was there when Morelli killed his wife's lover and he will come forward if he can be granted immunity." I explained.

"Holly shit Mike you got to be kidding me. Do you have any idea how long people have been waiting for this Morelli to screw up? So who is this guy?' Mark questioned.

"I don't know, but he will be calling me at exactly noon. From what this guy knows, I believe him."

"So what do you need from me? I don't have any choice but to get the district attorney involved no matter what, but I know we can definitely get him immunity if what he says is true." Mark promised.

"Well Mark get on it. It's 9:00 now, so we have less than three hours to come up with something before he calls back. I sure don't want to lose this connection to Dante." I said.

"I will meet you at your office in a couple of hours. We will listen to the call when it comes in together. Maybe I can catch something you might miss." Mark said.

The clock started to tick and it was moving fast, so fast I was finding it hard to breathe. I wasn't sure if it was lack of sleep, too much damn sugar or a combination of both that had me so jittery, but either way I was on edge and all I could do was prep for the call coming in at noon. So, I headed back to my office just as Morris called and explained that the phone call had been traced to a phone booth in the Hunter's Point District. He said he would go down and check it out to see if they could get some prints, though it was doubtful. I reasoned there would be hundreds of prints or it would be wiped clean, but at this point it couldn't hurt to take a look. "Ok Morris, but make it quick. Time isn't on our side. I need you for that incoming call at noon." I snapped frustrated.

As I walked into the darkness of my office, I sank into the comfortable chair with a resigned sigh. I was thinking somewhere in this huge mess of a case I needed to get a break. I had to get some answers. I knew I was getting close to who, what and where, but no "why". I could only hope this call would help to answer that question. I held my head in my one hand and rubbed the back of my neck with the other. I looked at the picture lying on my desk that Morelli gave me. I couldn't believe this was the kind of woman that would stray. Damn this case was consuming me and I turned the options over for what was probably the hundredth time in my mind. Could Dave have killed her for something he had done to her? Did Dante kill her for the same? Was there more to this case than meets the eye? Could Ellen have killed her thinking her husband was having an affair with her best friend?" I was second-guessing myself and as a detective that's never good. I closed my eyes from exhaustion for what I thought was a second, only to wake with a start when Morris ran into my office, nearly an hour later. I stared at the clock incredulously.

Morris had this huge contagious smile on his face and I caught myself smiling back and for some reason I was irritated with myself. "What the hell are you smiling at?" I barked.

"I think we know who our mystery caller is." Morris blurted. "Better yet we have video of the phone call he made to you. The store across the street has a sweeping surveillance system that caught it. It shows a man in a blue Lincoln getting out of his car and going into the phone booth exactly at the time the call was placed and terminated from the phone booth in the Hunter's Point District. And it gets better." His smile was nearly splitting his face in two and I was genuinely smiling back. Finally, a much needed break. "Yeah, when he left he closed the door behind him leaving his finger prints on the door. It doesn't get any better than that. Tom is down there right now collecting the samples. Hopefully we will know who this person is before he even calls you. Might just give us the ammunition we need."

I jumped up whacking him on the back, "Morris you made my morning. Hell you made my day. It's about time we actually get something we can go on. Thank you." I said appreciatively, but was interrupted as the phone started to ring. I checked the clock; it was too early. It was only 11:00 o'clock, but I still answered with hesitation. "Senetti here."

"Hey Mike this is Mark." I let the breath out that I hadn't even realized I was holding in 'til then. "I'm a few blocks away with an Immunity Decree from the District Attorney. So, we got what we need. I should be there in a few minutes to go over it, but I'm gonna need a huge favor for this one pal, which I will talk to you about when I get there."

I nodded "OK, just get here Mark, things are starting to fall into place."

"About damn time" he replied "on my way."

All the good news, in such a short amount of time, when it seemed we had nothing for so long gave me renewed energy. I felt the spirit in my step and had new hope. Maybe this battle could be won. I was ready for the next step, no matter what was to come. I knew with certainty that Morelli's hold on the city was weakening. I had always wanted this moment and yet now that it was within my reach, I didn't feel the satisfaction I thought I would. I knew he was guilty of Dave's death, but unfortunately, I also knew with every instinct I had, that he did not harm his wife. And with Dave's death, the disappearance of Alyssa had taken a back seat.

Thinking about Alyssa, my next thoughts naturally turned to Morelli. He wasn't going to take any of this lying down. He had a lot invested in all of this, his career and his life was at stake, but I knew with certainty he didn't give a damn about any of it without his wife. He had to be nearly insane by now. The news of Sal's death, Dave's body being found and Alyssa still missing, was a lot for one man to process, let alone the fact that he might be the cause of all of it. I was worried for the man that brought him down. Since we didn't really know who he was, I was nervous, because I needed to make sure this person was kept safe. It was only a matter of time before Morelli found out who the snitch was. He would stop at nothing to make sure he didn't stay alive.

CHAPTER 15

Morelli - Loyalty

9:10 A.M. and the phone is ringing. I pick it up hesitantly waiting on my end. "Is this Dante Morelli?"

"Yes who is this?" I cautiously ask.

"I just thought you should know that Sal was killed last night." The voice said softly on the phone.

My guts churn and I feel dizzy. My knuckles turn white as I grip the phone "Who is this?" I choke out hoping this is not real. Then all I hear is dial tone. I catch a glimpse at the man in the hall mirror barely recognizing myself. I look as if I have aged ten years. There's a lost look as I watch myself automatically dial Sal's number. This can't be true. I have always felt like Sal was indestructible. Is this some kind of trap? I wait for Sal to answer on the other end. He has to answer. With immense relief, I hear him pick up and I eagerly wait to speak to him, then I hear, "This is Sal. Leave a message." My heart plummets and numbness takes over as I hang up realizing I really shouldn't have called. Having a connection to Sal right now isn't a good thing. I feel defeated. My world is falling down around me. Alyssa, Dave, Sal. I have one recourse left. I dial Brian's number. I know he will be able to tell me if something really has happened to Sal. We all go back a long way. All those years ago growing up together had to count for something. I dial and wait.

"Hello."

I feel relief at the sound of Brian's voice. "B it's me, Dante. I just had the strangest call. Someone told me Sal is dead. That he's been killed. Tell me it isn't true."

"I'm at the morgue right now D. I just saw our friend. He's gone Dante." He said sounding as broken as I felt.

"Oh God Bri…."

"No Dante." He interrupted. "I don't want to hear anything, nothing from you anymore. This is the end. You can't call me ever again. There is only so much friendship can survive," he said sadly.

"But Bri…"

"No Dante." And the phone was dead.

I barely sense myself crumple and slide down along side of the wall as I begin to sob. We have been there for each other for as long as I can remember. The finality of his voice pierces me. I feel like I have died right along with Sal. It seems I have lost everyone that truly matters to me. I try to pull myself together. I have to figure this out. What am I missing? Why is this happening? My head throbs. I don't believe I have ever felt so empty. The only thing that makes me crawl to my feet is that I want answers. I stumble to the bar. I pour myself a drink and the liquor burns its way down my throat and into my empty stomach. I pour another before the burn in my stomach subsides. I am either going to drink myself into a numb stupor or find some answers in the bottle. I sit down on the stool to steady myself. I absently look at my phone and realize before I called Brian the last one I had talked to was Sal. "Fuck buddy what the hell happened." I cry out staring at my phone. Then I pick up the card Senetti left and though I hate asking anything from any man, I dial his number.

"Senetti here."

"Hi Mike, this is Dante Morrelli. You have a minute?"

"No not really why?" He asks his voice sounds guarded.

"I just heard my friend is lying in your morgue. Can you tell me what happened?"

"Yeah well I'm sure you mean Sal. I don't know much more than that. He came in late last night. He was found in the Sunset District. It will probably be all over the news this morning." And then with uncharacteristic sensitivity he said, "If it is any comfort, he didn't suffer. It was quick. I'm pretty sure he didn't even know it was coming. There was no struggle." I let out a ragged breath and he added, "I'm sorry for your loss."

"Thanks" I say and I meant it. "And my wife" I ask hopefully.

"As of yesterday we may have a few more leads, but nothing that I am at liberty to discuss until they pan out or the investigation is concluded." He finishes.

"Well thanks for nothing then." I say bitterly and hang up. I scroll down my calls and realize it was very probable that Sal had been killed right after he talked to me, since it had been late last night. What was it Senetti said "The Sunset"? Sal had never even left the city, which meant that Dave's body had never been destroyed. That left me wondering where Doc was? Did Senetti know where Doc was? Did he have him? My mind was racing? I had to make things happen. I punched the call in. How many times have I done things I didn't want to do? Once again circumstances left me no choice.

The ringing ended. "Hello."

"It's me."

"We heard."

"I think it was Doc. We need him..and fast. Call when you have something to tell me."

"Figured as much. Just waiting for the go ahead. We are on it. Be in touch soon." And the line went dead.

The life seems to be ebbing slowly out of me as I hang up. This is undoubtedly the first time in my life when I feel so hopeless, so helpless. My life is spiraling beyond my control. I have lost so much, so fast and feel like I can't do anything about it. I throw my tumbler across the room in frustration, but feel no sense of satisfaction as I watch it shatter to pieces. I reach over to pour myself another, and then I am engulfed in anguish. The tears stream down my face and I don't care. The only woman I can ever love is missing, probably dead; I have lost both my best friends, Dave is dead because of me... "Fuck" maybe it was all because of me...every fucking thing. I weep unashamedly. The torture I dealt Dave couldn't have been any more painful than what I was suffering now. I feel hollow inside. What is left? Nothing matters. It is that thought that pulls me out of the depths of despair. Since there is nothing to lose, I have to find out about my friend and my wife. I have to make someone pay. That's the only way I know how to get in control again. More people will have to die if that is what it is going to take. I am beyond caring.

The shrill ringing of my phone abruptly startles me from the dark plans I am brooding over. I grab the phone and snarl "Hello" and hear the new resolve in my voice, somewhere deep inside of me there is a tiny flame of hope still flickering.

"D?" The voice questioned.

"Yeah."

"We found him."

"And…?" I ask.

"Looks like he has a tail." He answered being careful not to mention any names.

"Well do what you need to do. Immediately. I don't know what has been said, nor do I give a fuck. Do we understand each other?"

"Can't be immediately. Looks like he is in spilling shit right now. Pretty sure he is in with counsel."

"Whatever you have to do, nothing leaves that mother fucker's lips. You can include his fucking counsel. Whatever it takes. I don't give a shit. You understand." Jesus was that me screaming in the phone? Where was the calm asshole? I felt like I was on a ledge ready to teeter over.

"Understood. Consider it done." The connection ended with a sudden click.

I knew now that one of the men I had always trusted to do whatever needed to be done was turning against me to protect himself. It was down to him or me and he was throwing me to the dogs. I didn't give a damn about what happened to me anymore, but I damn well wanted to see him pay for Sal. So let the killings continue. It didn't matter anymore. My rage was as out of control as my life.

I had one weakness in my life, the love for my wife. Someone knew that and was using it to destroy to me. I still couldn't stand the thought that something must have happened to her. But the thought that she might be alive somewhere was equally painful. I wiped away my tears with the back of my hand. No more tears. The time for crying was over. I knew that very likely I would not come out of all of this alive, so I sent a prayer up asking God to please forgive me for all that I had done and what I was about to do. I started making the calls. I put bounties on the heads of anyone that might have anything to do with Alyssa's disappearance. I rationalized Dave's death by telling myself that he had something to do with her disappearance. I pulled out every favor and called on anyone who feared me, and there were many to help on the path of my revenge.

I felt I had done everything for the moment and was ready to find something besides liquor to fill my stomach and a warm shower when the doorbell rang.

"Who is it?" I asked. I was surprised my voice sounded so calm.

"It's Ellen Dante." She sounded as sad as I felt and guilt washed over me.

I walked to the monitor and buzzed her in reluctantly. "Come in Ellen."

She was barely in the door before she threw herself at me crying. "Oh my God Dante I think Dave is missing now too or maybe he ran, because he was scared he was being blamed for Alyssa. I know they would never do anything. You have to help me Dante."

"Please Ellen." This was more than I could tolerate. She had no idea at the emotions raging inside of me. "I don't want to sound like a cold hearted bastard, but I can't even find my own wife right now. What makes you think I would have any better luck finding Dave," I lied, realizing she would soon know he had been savagely tortured and killed.

"Dante you don't believe that Alyssa and Dave could ever..." she began.

"Stop right there Ellen I don't want to even listen to that shit right now and you shouldn't either. I'm going to stay with the thought that they would never do that to us." The end of my sentence trailed off and the tears started all over again. Ellen wrapped her long thin arms around my neck and we clung together. My mind was tortured with the thoughts of Dave and Alyssa.

She leaned into me "Dante how could Alyssa's DNA have been in my bed? How? Unless..."

"Ellen everything points to it, I know, but I still can't believe it." I was remembering how Dave died never wavering in his answer that he had never been with Alyssa. I had to believe him. "I can't explain it, and I can't prove it Ellen, but I don't believe it." I uncomfortably tried to untangle myself from her embrace.

As Ellen stared into my eyes, I could see something. She was lying. Did she know more about our spouses than I did and she was keeping it from me just as I was keeping Dave's death from her? She saw something cross my face; possibly that I knew she was keeping something from me. Then she totally threw me off balance when her lips met mine in a hungry kiss. I was kissing her back before my brain registered. For just a moment I was kissing Alyssa. I could even smell Alyssa. Then reality swept in and I pulled back. I grabbed her by both arms and thrust her from me. "You have to leave, now... what the hell are you doing? Jesus what did I just do? I didn't even want to do that Ellen, I wasn't thinking."

"Dante don't you see we have been betrayed by the two people who we love most in the world? Why shouldn't we turn to each other?" She pleaded as she moved in again.

This time I backed away. "My heart belongs to Alyssa. I'm sorry Ellen. That kiss never even should have happened and I'm sorry it did." I gave her a quick, friendly hug and walked her decidedly to the door. I had done enough by killing Dave and I believed deeply it had been unjust, but I wasn't going to make another mistake by taking Ellen to bed. I would never sleep with her or anyone else.

CHAPTER 16

Senetti – Damning Evidence

The clock on the wall said 11:30. I had to look again at my watch just to double check. I felt anxious. I was about ready to meet the man that could finally put Dante Morelli behind bars, so it was little wonder I jumped as Mark came around the corner and sailed an envelope across the cramped office to land on my desk. "There you go my friend. A get out of jail free card signed by none other than Luis Alcosta the head District Attorney." Mark quipped waiting for my reaction.

I sat up straighter. Even though I was tired, and pissed that he could always aggravate the hell out of me, I wanted to kiss him right now. "Is that it?" I asked stupidly.

"What did you want a gold seal on it?" He answered.

He was a cocky little bastard, but he could weasel nearly anything out of anyone when he poured on the charm and he had probably used plenty getting this and was more than a just a little disappointed with my reaction. I allowed myself a slight grin at the thought of how I was thinking about kissing him, but would never let him know how happy this made me.

He took the smile as the small bit of appreciation I was going to show him and moved on. "So what time is our guy getting here? Mark asked.

"He should be here shortly. He said he would meet us here at twelve. And I am hoping he is a man who lives up to his word or you just went to a lot of trouble for nothing…but thanks" I added.

As if on cue my phone rang. We looked at each other and the excitement was tangible. This was it. I picked up the phone slowly as the tension mounted in the room.

"Senetti here."

"Mr. Senetti. I have a Mr. Blake Garlin here to see you."

"Send him up please. I'm expecting him." It took everything I had not to look or sound ridiculously silly, because I felt like jumping up and down. The best I could do was bounce out of my chair and go to the door and open it. I could barely contain myself. This was the man who watched Dante Morelli kill Dave Martin, and miraculously was alive to tell about it.

I watched a man walk down the hallway. He didn't seem from a distance the type of man that would be involved in any kind of murder, let alone someone who would work for Dante Morelli. As he got closer I could see he was dressed in a beautifully tailored suit, it spoke of money. He was clean cut, and sharp looking. He looked like a man who was all business. My stomach churned, this was not going to be good.

I put my hand out "Hello I'm Mike Senetti."

"Hello Mr. Senetti. Blake Garlin attorney for Dr. Mel Stevens." His handshake was strong. He was a man of professional confidence. "Mr. Senetti I apologize for any misunderstanding you might have since I am sure you planned on meeting my client in person, but I had to make sure everything was in place for his safety before he showed. I am sure you understand. I spoke to my client in detail before coming and explained to him his options. He has a great deal to lose here. He is reluctant to come in, but realized it might be his only chance for survival. At this point he can't trust anyone and after knowing the entire story I can see why he wouldn't."

I was trying to catch up. "Sorry Mr. Garlin and I don't want to be rude, but I'm not sure who you are, or who Doctor Stevens is and I'm only starting to get an inkling why you are here."

"No, I'm sorry Mr. Senetti. I should have made myself clearer. I am the attorney representing Dr. Stevens in regards to what transpired last night. I am here to make sure that what has been promised to him is legal and binding."

Until then no one who had been waiting in the room had made a sound. The tension was finally broken when Macenna said, "Does someone here want to tell me what the fuck is going on here?"

"I'm sorry and you are?" Mr. Garlin asked.

"I'm the assistant DA that's either going to save your client's ass or the one that's going to fry it." Mark was pissed and I could hear the aggravation in his voice that we were all feeling.

"Maybe we need to go to the conference room Mr. Garlin." I said trying not to let the disappointment show in my voice. We filed down the hallway and Morris was coming rapidly from the opposite direction. I knew he had something for me with just a glance. He had a look of expediency about him. "Have a seat, grab a cup of coffee and I will be right with you." I said motioning for Morris to meet me in my room.

"What's up Morris?" I asked.

"Well we found out who the prints belong to. They are the prints of Dr. Mel Stevens. I had them run him and it seems he has been picked up a couple of times for illegal gambling. You know where else we found his prints?" Morris said excitedly.

"Come on spill it." I said exhausted and not about to play guessing games.

"They were in the passenger seat of Sal's car. So he definitely was there when Sal was killed, since no other prints overlap nor do any others' exist in the car."

"Great work Morris. Now let's see what else we can find out about this guy." I said as I ushered Morris toward the conference room door.

"Gentlemen this is my colleague, Detective Morris from homicide. He will be joining us, since he is also part of this investigation." I said as I sat down facing both the attorney and the DA. So please let's start with you Mr. Garlin. You represent Dr. Mel Stevens and I believe he was the one that spoke with us a few hours ago explaining his situation and now here you are. What happened to our deal? He was supposed to come. I was supposed to talk to him." I said confused and more than a little annoyed.

"Mr. Senetti I apologize for any misunderstandings you might have since this is as new to me as you. I spoke to my client in detail before coming here and explained to him his options, but because of the situation he is in, you must understand his reluctance to come in and believe that he will walk out ok. He doesn't trust anyone. So, after speaking with him he will live up to his end of the deal if you live up to yours. I believe we are talking about full immunity from what he told me," Mr Garlin said.

"I'm sorry, but before I can give anyone immunity for a crime of this magnitude I would need to hear his side, in person, or he will have to write an affidavit. And how do you expect me to do that when he doesn't show Mr. Garlin?" Macenna said disappointedly.

"Well there are two options here, I have the video of Mel Stevens' confession of what transpired last night and I also have the tools used in the killing of Dave Martin as well as the scalpel that was used to kill a man that my client feels would have killed him if he didn't act defensively. The second option will be to sign the immunity in my client's name and I will make sure he turns himself in. As of right now he doesn't trust anyone, especially anyone or anything that has to do with Dante Morelli. So the ball is in your court gentlemen" Garlin stated.

"Well Counselor I would think he would be more worried about his life than his freedom. Turning himself in would be in his best interest, because after Morelli finds out he is alive and flapping his lips, he is going to do whatever it takes to keep him quiet." Macenna said.

"What I don't understand Mr. Garlin is why lawyer up if he had every intension of turning himself in if we give him immunity." I said.

"I advised my client that it was in his best interest to secure the immunity. He has what you need gentlemen." Garlin smirked.

"Is this worth your client's freedom?" Marcenna asked frustrated and I could hear the sarcasm in his voice. He was about as impressed with Mr. Hot Shot as I was.

I interrupted. "Let's just stop with all the bullshit and give us what you have so we can determine if what your client has is worth it. Does he have everything he said he had Mr. Garlin?"

"Mr. Senetti, he has that and more." Garlin said as he started to open his case to remove some item. He placed the first item on the table and it was in a clear plastic bag and through the plastic I could see a filet knife that had quite a bit of blood on it. Next, he pulled out another bag that had a small aluminum bat in it that also had blood splattered on it. As he was pulling his last bag out, I motioned Morris and told him to get Linda or Tom up immediately. The last item, seemed to be rags soaked in blood. I knew the son of a bitch was telling the truth. His client had been there and watched Dante pulverize Dave. My heart was racing. Finally this was coming to a close.

"So Mr. Senetti what we have here are some instruments that were used in the murder of the individual I believe you are investigating. The evidence you have before you is the blood of a recent homicide victim and you will find the bloody prints of Dante Morelli. My client was there that night as a doctor who was ordered to keep the victim alive in order that the torture could continue. Also, I have a scalpel that has my client's fingerprints, as well as another person's blood on it. This doctor who has come forward found he was to be executed next and this was an attempt to save his own life. "Do you think I have enough Mr. Macenna?" Garlin countered with more sarcasm than Macenna could have ever mustered.

"You have undeniably made your case Mr. Garlin, but without his testimony these instruments are irrelevant and I'm sure you know that. So, I need to hear it from him" Macenna said.

"I can do better than that, since I have his video testimony on my person to give to you when I get the Immunity Decree." Garlin said.

"We'll be back," Macenna said as he gestured me outside of the room.

As I watched Macenna walk out I followed close behind him with the anticipation of getting this doctor. It was exactly what I needed to get Morelli behind bars.

"So what do you think Mike?" Macenna asked.

"I think we have a gold mine sitting in front of us if it all checks out. I sent Morris to get Linda and Tom from the lab to get these bags tagged and tested as soon as possible. I see no reason why we can't give this man his immunity and give him protection as well."

"Yeah, I agree, but I would like to see the video." Macenna said.

As I started to head back into the room I saw Morris coming down the hallway with Linda and Tom from the crime lab.

"Hi Mike." Tom and Linda said in unison.

As we all walked in the room, I pointed out what items needed to be taken. I watched Tom and Linda gather the evidence and carefully place them in evidence bags and seal then for preservation.

"So Mr. Garlin, I am willing to give your client the immunity after I see the video of admission." Macenna said.

"I would be more than happy to play if for you if you can get a VHS player in here to play on the monitor that you have here." Garlin answered.

I asked Morris to go and get the video player that we used for interrogations. I was starting to get nervous that this man would disappear. As we all waited for the player to be hooked up, Tom and Linda put away all the items and Morris walked in to install the VHS recorder.

"Ok so is everyone ready?" Morris asked.

We all nodded ascent as Morris turned off the light and hit play on the remote. The picture sprang up before us. "Hello my name is Doctor Melvin Stevens and I was present the day Dave Martin took his last breath. My part in this murder was to keep Mr. Martin alive during the torture. I am not proud of any of my actions, but I had no alternative. I owed Dante Morelli. The bags that my attorney has in his possession will prove that Dante Morelli killed Dave Martin with those instruments. They will have Dave's blood and DNA as well as Dante's since I watched him bleed onto the knife that was used to finish Dave's life. The bat and knife also have the fingerprints of no one but Dante Morelli since he was the only one to use it. After the weapons were used Sal put them in a laundry bag and wrapped them up for disposal. Sal was also in charge of wrapping up Dave's body in heavy wrapping plastic. I can't tell you where this took place, because I was driven to the location blindfolded. I am sorry I don't know anyone else's name besides those I have mentioned. As we drove I could hear Dante talking to Sal before they removed my blindfold. Dante ordered me to get out of the car. He explained that all my markers were going to be washed away if on this night I did what he said. I was terrified for my life and I agreed, and I was hoping that if I lived I really would be free of this man and the slate would be clean. After the blindfold was removed I was led into a room and that was when I saw a man tied to a chair. I was desperate to get out of there, but I knew one false move and I would be dead. Dante called me into the room and asked me to sit in the corner. He told me he would call me when he needed me. Then I watched Dante ask the man tied to the chair about his wife's whereabouts with a quiet, yet deadly manner. Every time the man, who I later found out was Dave Martin, answered I watched Dante give a crushing blow to a separate part of his body, first one knee cap and then another, then his arms, he continued until there was just the crushed shell of a man left. I was there to make sure he did not die while he was questioning him. I was only asked once to revive him. By then his broken body and spirit didn't want to continue to live. I told Dante I could do no more to keep him alive. The more the man told him he didn't know anything about his wife the more vicious Dante became. Finally, Dave threw out some final words of defiance. There was no doubt in his mind he was a dead man and I don't know how he found the strength to even say them, but Dante picked up the filet knife and stuck it right underneath Dave's rib cage and he took his final breaths. So, there you have it gentlemen my confession and my part in what occurred the night Dave Martin was murdered."

As the video stopped playing the room was deathly silent except from the static on the television. We looked at each other in awe at what we had just heard. I felt sorry for the helpless man that was out there worried for his life. I watched Mark sign the Immunity Decree and he slid it over to Mr. Garlin.

"There you are Mr. Garlin. Your client has my word that he will get all the protection I can give him and immunity if he cooperates with the District Attorney's office. I just hope we can keep him from Morelli."

"So, Mr. Garlin now that you have your guarantees when can we get your client to come in?" I asked.

"I will make the proper calls so we can meet at my office for his surrender at 3:00 PM. Here is my card. It has the address. I'm a few blocks down the road. Thank you gentlemen for your time." Garlin said as he placed the Decree in his attaché case and walked out of the conference room.

"So, Mark where do we go from here?" I asked.

"I am going to go to the office and get a judge to get me a warrant for Dante Morelli. You go get our guy and keep him safe for the time being, because God help him if we don't get him behind bars before Morelli finds him." Mark replied.

"Sounds good Mark. I'll see you here around four o'clock and hopefully everyone will get some sleep tonight." I said. As I watched Mark leave the room I went over to grab the VHS tape out of the machine and I put it in my vault for safe keeping. This had already been a long day and my gut was rumbling. I asked Morris if he would like to join me for a late lunch before we went to Garlin's to pick up our guy.

CHAPTER 17

Senetti- Morelli's Blow

$\mathcal{M}$orris and I finished lunch quickly. I don't think either of us tasted our food. It was just something to stop the rumblings in our stomach and to fill the time until the meeting. When we were finished, I nodded and he understood it was time.

As we walked to the car I gave a sidewise glance to Morris and thanked him for all his help in this investigation.

"I'm just doing my job Senetti, but thanks, it means a lot to me that you appreciate the work I have done." Morris said looking at me over the patrol car before entering it with a smile.

As we started driving down the Mission district heading over to Bryant Street to meet our witness, I finally felt like we were getting close to finding out what happened to Alyssa Morelli. I had always felt like Dante's hands were dirty from the beginning, but wasn't sure, since his love for his wife seemed genuine. He may not have murdered his wife, but he certainly murdered Dave Martin and his arrest could possibly shed light on Alyssa's disappearance.

"Look there is our guy's vehicle right where he told us he would be" said Morris as he pointed out the Doc's car.

"Shit he's still in his car. Go around the block one time and park behind him. I want to make sure he goes up to Garlin's office. Wait drop me off around the corner to make sure he doesn't leave." I said excitedly.

As Morris pulled around the corner he asked "Why don't you leave me here and you drive around behind him to make sure it's really him. I'm faster on my feet than you are, no offense." He said with a slight smirk.

I realized the truth of his statement. He was younger and in decidedly better shape. Begrudgingly I acquiesced. "Fine" I hurried around the car to get into the driver's seat. As I left Morris there to watch, I saw what looked to be one of Morelli's goons getting into another car and quickly driving away. It struck me as strange, but without further thought I continued to hurry around the corner to make sure our guy was still there. I breathed a huge sigh of relief when I came around the corner to see his vehicle still there and Morris was keeping a close eye on the corner.

I pulled up behind his vehicle and could see that he was still in there. I placed the car in park and turned off the engine. I signaled Morris to make his way back to the car. I looked at my watch and it was a 3:00 o'clock. He continued to sit in the car and wasn't getting out to go up to Garlin's office as planned.

Before I could stop him, Morris startled me as he moved decidedly up to the car and opened the door. "Jesus Morris" I snapped at him frustrated as he jumped into my vehicle "Could you be a little more discreet." As good as he was going to be, and as hard as he worked, he still had a lot to learn.

"Senetti he isn't going anywhere calm down" Morris said with a smile on his face. "Just think Mike, tomorrow morning this will all be over and hopefully you'll get all the answers you've been looking for."

"Yeah, I guess you're right Morris sorry." I apologized. I looked at my watch and noticed it was ten after 3:00. I was starting to think the man was going to run if he thought for one minute that he could be killed, even after Morelli's arrest. Ten more minutes crawled by and he still didn't move.

"What are you thinking Mike?" Morris asked. He was getting as restless, as was I. We weren't men who liked to sit around.

"Well its 3:25, walk up and see if he's going to get out of the car." Maybe he is afraid to go on up, he might need an escort. I'll stay in the car in case he drives off. I'll also call a couple of units in for backup; it's hard to tell what this fool is thinking." I said

"Sounds good." Morris said relieved he could do something. He pulled out his badge attached to the chain around his neck to make sure it was in plain sight and hopped out of the car. I admired his graceful gait and quick feet as he approached the car. He walked slowly around the front. He cautiously approached the car with his hand on the grip of his holstered gun. He started to knock on the window.

Then, there was a moment of stark white and black followed by nothing. I heard sirens in the background and yelling voices that I couldn't recognize. "Can you hear me" a voice cried out? "We are going to get you out of the car, but I need you to stay as still as you can. I am putting this brace around your neck for support," the voice said.

As I tried to focus my eyes I realized I was staring at a multitude of emergency personnel around me as they carried me out of the car and into an awaiting ambulance. I was trying to answer their questions, but couldn't find the words or the vocal capacity needed to form the words. "What happened to Morris? Was he alright?" I could hear my thoughts, but could not make them into speech. As the ambulance sped away all I could think of was Morris. I looked up to recognize Linda from the CSI team and could see tears rolling down her face and knew from that moment that my young friend didn't make it. It overwhelmed me with sadness. My heart ached. I had no desire to voice the words any longer. I clinched my hands, and gritted my teeth. I felt Linda holding one of my hands and she looked down at me and words weren't needed. I closed my eyes, so I didn't have to look into hers.

She didn't say anything for a while, then as I felt the ambulance slow down she whispered "Mike, its Linda can you hear me?"

I tried once more to form the words my brain was screaming. I gathered all the strength I had left to answer her, but once again my brain went fuzzy and I mercifully felt blackness descend on me once more.

As I opened my eyes, I realized I was headed to the ER. The lights rolled by above me one after the other in the long hallway I was moving through. Linda was still there by my side running alongside the emergency team. I heard her explain to the ER physician what had occurred. "From what we can tell Morris and Senetti were investigating a suspect. We believe when Morris opened the car door to apprehend the individual in the car it set off an explosion killing Morris on the spot and causing severe damage to everything in its way, including Mr. Senetti here." Linda said.

I once again tried to focus all my energy into calling out to Linda. I saw her turn around and look straight at me as if she heard the unuttered words.

"Mike" she said "go ahead I'm right here."

I could only whisper "MORRIS he's...." Linda's expression said it all. She didn't have to repeat what I heard her tell the doctor. She gave a slight nod and the tears fell again. The anguish I felt was momentous, but it was subsiding into a blazing anger I never knew I could feel as I felt it overwhelm me. I had sent Morris up to the car. I had watched him as he gladly smiled at me and .....

"Rest Mike" Linda interrupted my thoughts. Then she was gone as the ER team moved in to do their work. The last thing I remembered was the bright lights above me and a warm sensation suffusing my body as I drifted into blissful unconsciousness.

When I slowly woke, I was aware of muffled voices before I could get my eyes to open. I knew instinctively I didn't want to wake, even though the nightmare I encountered still had not registered in my brain. Unfortunately, though I had lost all track of time, it was probably only minutes when it all hit me again. My eyes fluttered open to Linda, Tom and a few close friends from the Department who were in the room standing around the bed. "Hey" I croaked, glad that the words actually surfaced and I could hear them, though I didn't recognize my own voice.

Linda had obviously been sleeping in the chair next to the bed all night, she still clutched my hand and she looked wrinkled and worried. She stood and asked "Mike you awake?"

Searching for the words I replied slowly in my new raspy voice. "My eyes are open aren't they?"

"Shit he sounds like hell." Tom voiced what I was thinking as he stood over me.

Linda shot him a look, that warned him to shut up and he clamped his mouth shut. I looked over to Linda and asked again "Morris?" My eyes begged her not to tell me the truth, but I knew she would.

"There was absolutely nothing we could have done to save him Mike. That whole area was demolished. Whoever set the bomb knew exactly what he was doing; it was set to destroy everything and everyone. It was a miracle that you survived. We are on our way down there to sweep the crime scene. We wanted to make sure you were lucid first, because we wanted to know if you saw anything suspicious beforehand." Linda queried.

I searched in my memory. I saw Morris on the corner. I saw the man in the car. I...then I remembered I had thought I had seen one of Morelli's thugs leave the scene when we arrived. I relayed what I remembered. They nodded approval. Then I asked, "What did the Doctor say? How long until I am out of here? I have to get Morelli for this."

"Well right now it looks like you received a severe concussion from the explosion, a damaged eardrum and some facial cuts from flying debris, but overall you will, for the most part, recover." She knew as well as I did there are some things that never recover. "On another note Mike, Dr. Melvin was killed in the explosion as well. It looks like someone knew that he was going to be there. And if that isn't enough, Garlin's secretary found Garlin after the explosion with a slug in his temple." She gave it to me straight, holding back nothing and for that I silently thanked her. There was no softening the blow on any of it.

And though I knew the truth was the best approach, I was physically shaken. I knew it was bad, but this was more than I expected. Losing Morris was as bad as it gets, but if everything was gone, how could I hope to get revenge for his death. I fought for control as I whispered "If you don't mind guys I'd like to have minute with Linda alone." They nodded and left quietly wishing me well and warning me to get some rest.

When she was sure they were all out of earshot she softly asked "What's up Mike? What do you need? You know I will do anything."

"I need a huge favor from you. I know it is asking a lot with all that's transpired in the last twenty-four hours, but I know I can count on you. The tape that shows the Doc's testimony needs to be moved to a safer place. The only thing that's going to put that son of bitch Morelli away is the Doc's confession. And if he finds out that there is a taped confession, he will get to it. There is no telling what he will do, or who he has under his control. We can't let Morris's death be in vain. That son of a bitch needs to pay for what he's done. His wife's disappearance does not atone for everything else he has done," I said spitting the words out in a fury.

"Sure thing Mike, you know I will do it, and you know you can trust me, but you need to rest and quit working yourself up. It's not good for you right now. I'm assuming you put it in your office safe. I will need the combination."

"I don't want to write it down. I want you to memorize it." No one has the combination, but me, and now you. I need this done before you do anything else this evening." I relayed the combination to her and she repeated it quickly and efficiently. I nodded and she started for the door. I grabbed her hand "be careful and thank you for being there for me." My voice cracked as a mixture of emotions raged through me.

"Ah Senetti don't ruin your mean streak, you have everyone fooled." Then she lowered her voice to a near purr "I've always known you were a softy." She said as she winked "Don't worry all your secrets are safe with me." She gave my hand a final squeeze and walked out the door with a flirtatious smile running into the doctor that was walking in.

"So what's the verdict Doc?" I asked as I leaned up looking for my clothes.

"Well you have some superficial injuries, nothing that won't heal with some rest, but my concern is your head injury, which resulted in a severe concussion. So we'd like to keep you for the remainder of the night for observation and run some more tests in the morning, just to make sure there is no swelling." He replied with that professionally detached, yet concerned voice doctor's reserve for patients.

"Well thanks for your concern Doc, but that's not going to happen" I said as I swung my legs over the edge of the bed. "I have to get out of here if I'm going to catch the person responsible for this crisis that I feel I have at least in part created. So if you could be so kind as to find my clothes, I would be much obliged." I started to stand, but immediately found myself seated on the edge of the bed, partially because my vision blurred and my ears were ringing and partly because the doctor put his arm on my shoulder, gently but persistently forcing me to stay still.

The Doctor peered at me for a few minutes before he handed me my clothes off the hook in a closet and replied, "You don't remember me do you? You met me a few years back."

I looked closely at him trying to recall how I had met this man before. "I can't recall your face, but your voice sounds familiar" I said unsure. And that's when I did remember the last time I saw this man in front of me. "Holy shit" I whispered as I put my clothes down and leaned back on the bed.

Chapter 18

Senetti - Remembering

My words sputtered out of me as I stared at the doctor who tried to save my wife years before. I thought I had buried the memories and with it the pain that I felt searing through me once again. For a brief moment I felt the pain Dante was feeling for the loss of his wife. "Yeah Doctor Johnson, I remember".

Seeing him took me back to the night that altered my life irrevocably. I could still see the laughter on her face. She glowed and was truly stunning in her evening gown. She was nervous and excited for the awards ceremony where she would be receiving recognition. I should have been happy for her and I was proud of her for her accomplishments, so for her sake I smiled at my beautiful wife as I tried to stifle my alter life of solving crime. I should have been ecstatic, as I had just solved the murder of a twelve-year-old boy who had been murdered by his father. I had put the son of a bitch behind bars, but somehow I still felt that was too easy for him as I remembered the battered body of his small son. To continue the charade and put up a good front, not wanting to spoil the night for my wife, I ordered one drink after another, with little help at alleviating my brooding thoughts. There was something about that defenseless, little man lying broken on the floor at the brutal hands of his father that touched my heart. If only I could have saved him. If only someone had taken the time to report the repeated bruises and broken bones on his tiny, emaciated body. I had seen other cases of abuse, other murders, but the innocence on the child's face struck something in me and I couldn't let go of the thoughts crowding my mind throughout the exquisite dinner that seemed tasteless, the entertainment I had no interest in and the ceremony that drug on. I continued to paste a smile on my face and I continued to drink, waiting for the end of the evening. Finally, after many congratulations and even more photo shoots my wife said we could go home.

I gave my stub to the valet and waited patiently for the car to arrive. My wife, always sensitive to my every mood, asked if there was anything wrong as she touched my face with a concerned looked. I lied and told her nothing was wrong and changed the subject by telling her how proud of her I was, which was not a lie.

As the car approached, I leaned to open the door for her and kissed her on the cheek before she sat in the front passenger seat. I don't know how it happened. I was driving too fast, the roads were icy, the alcohol slowed my motor skills, I never checked her seat belt. It could have been a dozen reasons, all for which I blamed myself, but the fact is the car skidded off the road and the strange thing is it barely suffered a dent, nor me a scratch, but my wife in her excitement from the evening's festivities had neglected to buckle her seat belt and was thrown from the vehicle and though she looked to be only sleeping with barely a bruise on her, I knew something was wrong as she struggled to look at me. I dialed 911 and held her hand. The ambulance arrived in minutes that seemed like hours. I just knew she would be fine. She was talking to me. She told me her chest hurt, so maybe she had a broken rib. Since she was in the medical field, I figured she had a pretty good idea what was wrong. I left the car refusing to let her go to the hospital alone. I told her I loved her and apologized repeatedly. When we got to the hospital she assured me she would be fine. I kissed her on the cheek as she was whisked away into the emergency room. I waited outside the door, figuring they would have her patched up in no time. Instead, the doctor came out less than a half hour later. I still remember it with crystal clarity. Still garbed in his surgical gown the doctor came out of the ER "Mr. Senetti?"

"Yes, how's my wife?" I asked.

"I'm Doctor Johnson and I am so sorry to have to tell you this, your wife had a fractured rib and it pierced her heart." He said gently and compassionately with his hand on my shoulder.

My knees buckled. Disbelief coursed through me. When I could find my voice I looked up at the kind man and his assistant kneeling beside me. "Can I see her?" I asked. I still couldn't believe it. It had to be some sick joke.

"Sure". He answered helping me to my feet. I felt like an old man as I tottered through the door.

He took the sheet off of her beautiful face. It was flawless. I couldn't believe she was gone. There was no blood, no bruise, not even a scratch. How could this happen? How could she be gone? Needless to say that was a dark time in my life when I went through bouts of depression, but I never touched a drink after that night and I still blamed myself for her death.

Once again I raised my eyes to the kind doctor who stood before me. "Yes Doctor Johnson I remember everything" I whispered as he nodded, patted my shoulder and walked out of the room.

I reached over to get my cell phone and called Linda. I knew every moment I spent here Dante was manipulating whoever and whatever he needed to in order to get away with murder.

"This is Linda," she answered on the second ring.

"It's Mike, I need a huge favor and please don't give me any shit." I said

"Sure what's up" she replied?

"I need you to come get me." I said

"Do you think that's a good idea Mike?" she asked with concern.

"All I can say is that I'm not going to let Morris's death be in vain. For every minute we waste this son of a bitch is scheming on how he's going to beat the rap. He now knows we know he was there for the murder and I'm betting he will do anything to stay out of prison."

"Fine, where do I meet you," she replied sarcastically.

"I'll be waiting in the front of the main entrance of the hospital. Did you get the videotape? I asked.

"Yeah, I have it in hand as we speak. And I need to get the hell out of here anyway, it's crazy here in the station with the news on Morris's death." she said.

"Be careful, that tape is the only thing left linking this bastard to the all these deaths." I replied.

"On my way" she whispered, "too many ears here anyway."

I painfully got dressed in what was left of my soot stained clothes. Taking a glance in the mirror, I blanched at the man who stared back at me. I looked like a walking dead man. Dead....once again my mind drifted back to my dead wife. I can almost relate to this murdering fuck in his love for his wife. It would push a man to do just about anything. I started for the front of the hospital, hoping no one would look too closely at my disheveled appearance. Hopefully, Linda was there, because I was pushing my luck with this little escape. I walked slowly through the hospital towards the entrance and the memories hit me like a fist in the gut. It was as if that night was happening all over again, and I wanted a drink badly for the first time in six years. I stumbled to the front of the hospital, enveloped in waves of grief. Pushing my way through the wrenching memories I saw Linda pull up as the glass doors opened. I hobbled to the car as she reached across the seat and opened the passenger door for me to get in. I gritted my teeth and my body tensed as I bent to get in and the pain shot through every nerve in my body. Finally, I sank into the seat, wiping the sweat off my brow.

Linda glanced over at me and tried to hide the shock I could see on her face at my appearance. "You look like shit Senetti. This is probably one dumb ass idea." She said.

"Almost as beautiful as you." I replied shakily as the pain subsided a bit.

"So, where to handsome?" She asked, always having to have the last word.

"Bitch" I whispered as she smiled. "Take me to my house. So I can shower and get out of these stinking clothes."

The rest of the ride to the house was quiet. I leaned my head back and just let the warmth of the sun sink into my bones and the music relax me as I shut my eyes. My mind drifted to Morris. I felt guilty once again for someone else's death. He had all the potential of a great cop. As I reclined further into the seat, trying to close off all my thoughts, I drifted into a haze of blurred images. Just as I started to doze I sat up straight as those indistinct figures took shape. Something hit me. What was it?

I looked at Linda my eyes wide. "Oh my God Linda" I mumbled looking across at her. Was there something to this or was it because my mind had been dwelling on my wife? Could there be a connection? Did my wife and Alyssa cross paths that night? What the hell was it that my mind was trying to focus on?

"What? What is it?" Are you going to be ok?" she asked worriedly pulling into my drive.

"Help me out of this car and I will try to explain what I don't even understand myself." I said wincing again at the fresh assault of pain as I tried to crawl out of the car, thankful for her help.

She looked at me hopefully, as she physically moved me from the car. "You are on to something. I can see it. What is it?"

"Hold on." I breathed catching my breath as I struggled to navigate the steps, leaning heavily on her. She was amazingly strong for such a small woman.

Once inside I fell into a chair and she hurried to get me a glass of water. "There are pain pills in the cabinet above the sink." I yelled. She came back with them and I gave her a thankful glance as I gulped them down.

"Now what?" she asked anxiously.

"In my desk, in the middle drawer, there is a folder. It is right on top. You can't miss it." I replied as I waited for the pills to take effect.

She was back in minutes. I reluctantly opened the folder holding all the photos that were taken the night that my wife died.

"Fuck, fuck, fuck I knew it." I began with a whisper and ended screaming.

"What! Jesus what is it?" she asked straining to see the picture in my hand.

I turned over a photo and handed it to Linda.

"Oh my god Mike." She barely replied as she looked first at the photo and then at me as it all began to sink in.

"That's right Linda. My wife knew Alyssa. Why in the hell didn't I see it before? If I wouldn't have seen Doctor Johnson and that damn hospital it might not have even clicked now." I said as I scrutinized the picture. "The assistant that helped doctor Johnson that night, if I'm not mistaken was Ellen."

"Jesus" she muttered.

"Call doctor Johnson and ask him if he remembers her working for him and if she was on with him that night" I commanded.

"On it" she said as she reached for her phone and took another look at the picture.

"Look Mike isn't that Dante and Dave in the background?" Linda asked, pointing a finger at the two figures laughing behind the two beautiful women.

"Fuck if it isn't. Jesus Linda how did my wife know her? What was the connection?" My head was swimming with possibilities, none of which made any sense at all.

"Linda, I want a background check on my wife and Alyssa. Make the connection and get back to me." I felt myself wavering on the brink of a deep chasm of grief. I couldn't fall into it now. "I just need a minute alone". She didn't move. "To think." I added.

"You don't look so good Mike. I'm not sure I should leave you alone." She said, reaching for my hand.

I grasped it like a dying man. "It's ok, go. I have to get to the bottom of this." I said as I regretfully let go of her hand.

"Ok, I will get on this, but I will be back soon."

She started to leave, bent down and kissed the top of my head and said, "I'm here if you need me and I mean that Mike, however you need me." Then she slowly walked away and I heard the door softly close behind her.

I almost called her back. I didn't want to be alone with my thoughts, but it was as if my wife's death had happened all over again. I felt like I was breaking into pieces. My entire body screamed, but the physical pain was preferable to the anguish I was feeling. I painfully pushed myself up from the chair. I went into the kitchen and rummaged through the cabinets to find the bottles of liquor right where I had left them years before. My hand shook as I lifted a bottle to my lips and felt the liquor burn its way to my aching gut.

CHAPTER 19

Senetti – Ties

Something was eating away at me even more than the liquor, what was it? My mind was whirling. There was something I was missing, but what was it? My brain though fuzzy was working to sort out some detail that would tie everything together. Fuzzy or not, I knew I had no intention of only taking one drink. I tipped the bottle repeatedly feeling the welcome, steady burn that numbed my aching body and dulled the pain in my head and heart. My body felt like liquid, and my mind blurred even more. The liquor on top of the pain pills made my world spin out of focus, but just before blackness slowly descended I saw Ellen and my wife, but it wasn't at the party, it was in the hospital the night she died. Jesus was I just seeing these women everywhere? I tipped the bottle again hoping the liquor would renew some memory I didn't know I had. I awoke to Linda leaning over me yelling my name. I tried to focus. I had no idea how long I had been on the floor; I only knew my mouth felt like sandpaper and my head hurt like a son of a bitch.

"Quit the fucking yelling" I mumbled.

I saw her fear turn to anger "What the fuck Senetti, you haven't been through enough shit in one day? You want to drink yourself to death now. How fucking stupid are you?" She yelled the last sentence just to feel better.

"And you saved the day why?" I asked still not daring to sit up.

"You told me to come back when I had the background matches or did you forget that too? You needed time alone….. to think. You're thinking alright, thinking of taking another drink."

I struggled to sit, every muscle in my body screaming. She could have helped me, but she stood back in satisfaction, hoping the pain of my body reached the stupidity of my head. I got up on all fours and crawled to a chair. She finally took pity on me and helped me into it.

Her voice softened a bit "Seriously Mike what were you thinking?"

"I didn't want to think" I answered and my eyes begged her not to ask me any more questions.

"I didn't want to think, but that's all I did, and the liquor helped me remember." I said as she looked at me skeptically.

I swear before I passed out I saw Ellen with my wife that night at the hospital."

"What the hell are you talking about? You just saw the picture of Ellen and Alyssa at your wife's party, that's why you dreamed it. It wasn't the damned alcohol."

I instantly felt a burning rage. What the hell was going on? This whole thing was fucking up my life on more levels than one. Too many people had died, among them a very good man. And if any of these assholes were involved in my wife's death, and I had blamed myself all these years then God help them. Someone had to pay and I was going to start with Morelli.

I could hear my phone ringing in the living room. I had left it near my gun on the mantle. I tried to answer it, but at the pace I was moving I would never get there to stop the insistent ringing. I sent a pleading look at Linda and she reluctantly got up to answer it.

"It's Mark" she said with a sense of urgency as she tossed me the phone

"Hello" I answered.

"Hey Mike" he said and he sounded excited.

"Give me some good news please" I asked hoping I hadn't read him wrong.

"I got it" he nearly shouted.

"Got what?" I asked.

"I have in my possession an arrest warrant for Dante Morelli on capitol murder charges stemming from the death of one Dave Martin. We are also in the process of trying to link him to the deaths of the Doc, his attorney and Sal. Whether he directly killed them or not is of no consequence, their deaths are an indirect result of his actions.

"Man if you were here right now I would kiss you" I said nearly laughing, though realizing it hurt too much settled for grinning as if it would split my face.

"Well pucker up, because the boys and I are on our way to the hospital to pick you up though I could dispense with the kiss sweetheart" he joked.

"I'm actually at home" I informed him.

"What the hell. How did you manage that?" He asked and I could hear his disappointment that he wouldn't be the one to spring me. He loved playing the hero.

"Linda and I will meet you at Morelli's. And she can kiss you for me how's that?" I said as I hung up.

"What's going on Mike?" Linda asked hearing her name.

"They got the arrest warrant for Dante" I said still smiling as I reached for Linda to support myself as I struggled to sit and then stand.

As I got up slowly to my feet, the pain seared through me. I barely felt the shower I had so looked forward to and I put my clothes on as quickly as I could considering every movement was painful and I was getting stiffer by the minute.

As Linda and I headed out the door I shook my head I still couldn't get the picture of Alyssa, Ellen and my wife out of my head. What was the connection? As I was climbing into the car, on instinct, I asked Linda to run back into the house and get the picture on my desk. She nodded as though the thought had already entered her mind. I had slowly and thankfully just sank into the seat and Linda was already back with the picture in hand.

She handed me the picture smiling. I couldn't help but smile myself and feel this was all coming to an end. Although nothing good comes from someone's death, it was good to know the person responsible was never going to hurt anyone again and that was satisfaction enough for me.

As we pulled up to Morelli's address, I noticed his gate was open and every light in the house was lit, it was almost majestic as it blazed with lights.

"Stay here." I said as I struggled to get out of the car.

"Don't you think we should wait Mike?" She asked anxiously.

"I'm not letting this son of bitch get away." I clipped my words off angrily.

"Mike... Mike slow down," she said as I started to walk towards the house. And had the situation not been so intense I would have laughed, because I was surely moving at a turtle's pace.

I could see Dante sitting on the couch drinking through the huge plate glass window that over looked the bay. I walked slowly up to the house with my hand near my side arm, knowing that anything was possible with Morelli. The closer I got to the front door the more I could hear my heart beat with anticipation. I was finally going to put this man away. As I reached for the handle I noticed the door was ajar and I heard "I can't believe it took you this long Senetti." It was Dante's voice, but it was slurred until it was nearly unintelligible.

As I continued to push the door open, I could see Dante slouched into his living room couch. It shook me to my core as I looked at this shell of a man. He bore little resemblance to the hardened well-dressed man I came across a few days ago. Of course the last couple of days, since I had met Dante, had done little for my appearance either I reminded myself.

"Sit down and let me tell you a story." He slurred waving towards a seat.

I couldn't help but do as he asked; since I truly wanted to hear anything he had say. I stumbled to the ottoman opposite him that he indicated. Between us was a table with a decanter of Scotch. He refilled his glass and poured one for me as if he had known I was coming. What he didn't know is that I turned on my cell phone, so Linda could hear the conversation.

"You know I did love her." He stated matter of fact as he glared at me

"You talk about her in the past tense as if she were dead." I replied.

"No No, I talk about her as if I'll never see her again. Since you and I know I'll never be able to get out of the mess that I've created here. Let's just say death will become me, since without her my life has no meaning." When he spoke of her his voice was nearly reverent and I believed him.

"You got one thing right Morelli. Your life as you know it is over. You will pay for Dave and Alyssa. But most of all you will pay for

Morris. I could give a fuck about your cronies. Doc and Sal probably deserved what they got. But you do not have the right to say who lives and dies." I replied bitterly.

"So what now?" He asked as he finished his drink with one gulp.

"Well now you go to jail for the rest of your miserable life. While there you get to relive the horrible things you've done over and over again. And then if you're lucky, just maybe you'll find you have a soul. Finally, you will rot in hell." I said with some satisfaction as I reached over to place the handcuffs on the coffee table.

"You really think I'll only get life?" He asked sarcastically as we both turned to see the parade of cop cars driving up and surrounding the house through the window.

"I take it that line of flashing lights is in my honor." He said with a smile as he grabbed the handcuffs and started to put one on his left wrist.

I relaxed a bit as he placed the first cuff over his left wrist resignedly. An unfortunate mistake on my part, because with no warning he pulled out a 45 and point blank shot me in the chest. I fell back hearing Linda screaming my name through the phone. I watched him calmly put on the other cuff, but not before throwing the gun on the couch as he walked out the front door fully composed.

He turned back only once at the threshold, "Now you can truly feel the pain I'm feeling." he said as closed the door behind him.

CHAPTER 20

Dante- The Arrest

At that point I believed everyone should feel the pain I was feeling and my sole purpose was to cause it. Right or wrong it gave me some kind of satisfaction and left me feeling less lonely. I would never see the woman I loved again, and the fact that I was being blamed made me careless, I wanted to strike out at the world, hurt, maim, kill anyone and everyone.

I heard the commands to drop to the ground come from everywhere and for a fleeting moment I thought of charging into the midst of them and letting the bullets riddle my body to get it over with. My death couldn't come soon enough. I spent a moment too long considering it through my alcohol infused mind and found myself forced bodily to the ground.

As my body was crushed to the pavement I faintly heard Mike yell from inside the house. "Where is that son of a bitch?" I couldn't help but smile when they stood me up to change the direction of the cuffs. I knew if I had wanted to kill the bastard I would have done so a long time ago, but I had hoped that he would find out what happened to Alyssa. However, his Achilles heel was his arrogance, and this deserved a little stinger from me before I was sent away, besides he had miserably failed if he still thought I killed my wife.

"Mr Morelli. I'm Mark Macenna with the States District Attorney's office. You have the right to remain silent. Anything you say or do may be used against you in a court of law. You have the right to consult an attorney before speaking to the police and to have an attorney present during questioning now or in the future. If you cannot afford an attorney, one will be appointed for you. Do you understand what I'm telling you? You worthless piece of shit. Now, get him the hell out of here."

That was the last moments of my freedom. I no longer cared nor was I worried about the outcome. The truth is I should have been jailed long ago or worse dead, but throughout the years I learned that the love I had with Alyssa was more important to me than the power I wielded over others. My love for her was enough that I felt myself changing for her. And the strange part was, I had found I was a better, happier, person. Though it did me little good I realized, as I was being led to the patrol car that would lead me to my final days.

As they guided me into the patrol car's back seat and buckled me in, I couldn't help but close my eyes to recall some of the good days that were behind me once again.....

"Quit starring" I told her as I woke up next to her.

"Pretty hard to do Mr. Morelli" She replied.

"Well then good morning Mrs. Morelli" I told her as I rolled her on top of me and kissed her softly.

"I can't believe we did it" she replied kissing me over and over and over.

"Yes we did, any regrets?" I asked.

"None yet, but the day is still young" she said happily as she continued kissing me.

"How did I end up being the luckiest man on the planet? Last night will forever be the best day in my life." I said seriously.

"Well remember what the priest said last night. 'Till death do us part. I couldn't think of anyone else in this world I would rather spend the rest of my life with." She said as she laid her head on my chest.

"Morelli we're here wake up" the cop said as we pulled into the precinct full of waiting officers.

They looked like a pack of wild wolves ready to pounce on a deer. I expected the worse since I knew shooting Mike and having one of their own killed was not going to get me any special treatment.

As they walked me down the halls of 850 Bryant precinct to start the booking process, I could see Brian coming down the hallway. It was like slow motion watching Brian taking his best shot at me. As he wound up again making sure he made point.

"That was for Sal, Morris and Mike." He whispered as he helped me back up from my knees and then brushed off my shoulder.

I knew I had it coming. Hell I knew today was going to be one of the longest in my life. But to me she was worth the pain and I would do it all over again if I had to, but it was like a wall of mirrors. Every time I thought I could figure out who killed my wife I hit another wall. I knew Senetti had, more information and I had to find a way to get it in order to find out what happened to Alyssa before I died. I didn't want to die in vain.

"This way." the officer said as he directed me into a cell. "Kneel while we take the cuffs off" he said and I noticed the crowd of cops growing behind him.

As the cuffs came off I felt the first of many kicks to my back that made me fall face forward. One by one they lined up to get a piece of me. The funny thing is I didn't even give a shit. All I could think was "bring it on, go ahead finish me off." However, they figured that was too good for me and only beat me into unconsciousness. When I came to they repeated the "Brotherhood ritual." Yes even the pricks have one. I knew the lines I had crossed had consequences and that I would pay, but I also knew they wouldn't let me die now as I slipped into blackness...........

"Wake up its not time for you to leave me" I could hear the voice I loved most sobbing.

As I starred around trying to figure out where I was, I noticed the IV's in my arms and could see her crying from the corner of my eyes. The pain I felt from watching her tears were worse than the physical pain I was feeling.

"Oh you're a sight for sore eyes." I said slowly and painfully.

"Oh my God I thought you left me. I love you so much" She said tearfully as she squeezed my hand and reached over to kiss me.

"I love you too and I'm not going anywhere. I'll always fight to stay with you" I replied.

"I don't know what I would have done without you." She said.

"What happened?" I asked.

"You left the party early since you weren't feeling well. And apparently you passed out and crashed into some parked cars." She replied.

"Good thing the hospital knew you were my husband and called me right away. I'm just so glad that you're ok" She replied with a worried look on her face.

"Well I'm glad you're here with me. I love you." I whispered while grasping her hand.

"Is there something you want to tell me?" She asked.

"About what?" I replied. I was so damned confused. How the hell did I get in the hospital? Where had she been? What was going on?

I could see her unfolding a piece of paper. "This was found in your wallet while they were trying to identify who you were." She said as she started to unfold the letter.

On the outside I saw my handwriting and it read "In case of emergency please make sure my wife (Alyssa Morelli) gets this."

Then she began reading in barely a whisper "My Sweet Alyssa... If you are reading this I am gone, but I can't leave this world until I have told you once more how important you have been in my life. Thank you for letting me be a part of the incredible journey that was us. Knowing you is the best thing that could have ever happened to me. I never knew how empty my life was before you were in it. For that I will be forever grateful. I will carry our love to the grave and will always remember how great we were together. Love you always. Dante."

I knew it was the letter I always carried on me in case something happened to me. I couldn't imagine leaving her, but if I did I had to proclaim my love to her one last time. I wanted to explain that she was only supposed to read that after I was gone, but the words wouldn't come, I felt myself sink into a dark tunnel once again. I willed my eyes open to look at her again and words weren't needed, as my vision went from blurred to black I saw her cross her fingers, our sign, our signal of us. She kissed her fingers and I felt them pressed to my lips as my world faded away.

The sweetness of the moment was gone as fast as it came, as a rough voice intruded "Morelli wake up, your attorneys are here." My mind scrambled to make sense of it all. What the fuck was going on? Where was Alyssa? I didn't even know what was real anymore.

No it wasn't a dream, but I was right back to the same nightmare. I opened my eyes to find myself lying in a shit hole of a holding cell. God I wished myself back to the hospital room.

I stood slowly to my feet, trying not to show them that they had got the better of me for once. I calmly brushed myself off and turned around so they could once again place the cuffs on me. They tried to inflict as much pain as possible by man handling me, but I took some satisfaction in not showing them anything, the physical pain was nothing to the emotional pain I was feeling.

As they escorted me to an interview room where my legal team was waiting, I could see Senetti sitting at the end of the table with his arm in a sling and beside him was the one that had read me my rights. They all stood when I walked into the room as the officer removed the handcuffs and sat me down at the end of the table.

"Jesus Christ Dante what happened to you" one of the attorneys commented after noticing my battered body

"I believe I fell during the arrest" I replied as I sent a cocky smile Senetti's way. I wouldn't let him know every single part of my body was screaming with pain, nor would I rat on him. It would infuriate him that I could stand up to whatever he dealt out and yet not say a word.

"Ok let's cut the bullshit. You know why you're here and we are ready to give you the deal of a life time. And I mean deal." Macenna said and I could hear the irritation in his voice.

"And what would that be? You got nothing I need or want. I tried your way and all you did was point me in the wrong direction. I can't reverse what happened. You put me here not me" I replied pissed off more than ever. The anger felt good, it helped rid me of the ache I felt inside and out.

"How about we spare your life in exchange for information on the whereabouts of your wife? Yes for all the damage you've caused I'm willing to spare your life and seek life in prison in place of the death sentence. We just need to know what happened to her. Everything points back to you Dante. There is no one else. So think about what I just offered you. If not I'm going to charge you for the murder of Dave, the Doc and Morris. And the attempted murder of Senetti. And I hold all the cards. You know I'll win." Macenna said confidently.

"Now wait a minute here. We aren't going to sit around here while you trash our client with all these accusations. The mere fact that you have our client in custody over some factored evidence is appalling." My attorney shot back.

"Well counselors play your cards, because at this point I don't give a shit what you do. I have nothing to lose anymore. So take your best shot." I replied knowing at that moment then they had no clue where she was and neither did I and that caused me a whole different kind of pain. I could no longer do what was needed to find her and that made me feel helpless, a feeling I could not relate to.

I watched them all rise and leave the room to discuss what the actual charges were going to be, but regardless of what it was, I just didn't care. I'm a realist; I knew my life as I knew it was over.

CHAPTER 21

Morelli – Justice Served

*N*ovember 10ᵗʰ 1997, seven months had come and gone in that rat hole of a cell. I had suffered every indignity that guards and inmates could inflict on me short of actually killing me. I had become numb to every abuse, even the thought of killing myself held no appeal. The only thing that kept me going from day to day was the hope that something or someone would come up with information on my wife. However, I now knew I had run out of time, I would go to my death never knowing what happened to her. Today was the start of the end of my life. I sighed and squared my shoulders; I was ready to take whatever they gave me. I had wasted everything in vain trying to figure out what happened to my love.

As I was escorted from my holding cell to the courtroom, I could hear the anticipation of my arrival; it sounded as if a swarm of bees were buzzing around my head. As they guided me through the courtroom doors, the room became deathly silent. The courtroom held only a hundred to two hundred people, but it was packed to capacity with on lookers standing in the wings. It looked as if everyone awaited my downfall. The stares of every spectator were focused on me and the hatred was almost tangible. It was as if it penetrated my very being. I sighed, and if it was the last thing I would do, I wouldn't let them know that this well, groomed man felt their hostility. I would never stoop to that, even when I walked to my execution, which I knew was only a matter of time. While the bailiffs sat me down and removed the handcuffs from my wrists, my attorneys patted me on the back to reassure me I was going to be ok. I actually felt myself smirk, I knew it was never going to be ok, the price I was going to pay would, without a doubt, be my life.

As the D.A. started his opening arguments my thoughts, as always, drifted to my wife. I felt as if I were being prosecuted for more than the murders I committed, it was as if I was guilty of actually loving someone more than myself. It was ironic that the one good thing I did in my life was going to be my downfall.

I tried to focus on the case being presented. "Good morning ladies and gentlemen of the jury." He said. Then he accusingly pointed at me and I snapped my head up and looked him straight in the eye. His eyes met mine and his voice rang through the courtroom "Dante Morelli is a killer. The evidence in this case is incontrovertible. It will prove that the people in this world who think they know this man best, know him the least. On the night of March 19th Dante Morelli took it upon himself to question one of his best friends in the disappearance of his wife Alyssa Morelli. Not getting the answers he wanted, Mr. Morelli tortured his friend Dave Martin in a vicious onslaught with a bat, breaking every bone in his nearly unrecognizable, mangled body. During the torturing of Mr Martin an eyewitness, Dr. Stevens was present to bring Dave Martin back to consciousness, to answer questions and prolong the beating. Once he realized he was not getting the answers to confirm his suspicions that Dave Martin and Alyssa Moreilli were engaged in an affair, since Dave Martin was innocent, he butchered Mr. Martin with this knife". He held the bloody knife up for the jury. "And this knife, by the way, had Dante Morelli's finger prints on it. This barbarous act led to a chain of events that left not one, but five dead bodies among those bodies are: that of Scott Morris a San Francisco police officer, Dr. Mel Stevens and his attorney were also among those who were unfortunately killed, but since he was an eyewitness and coming forward and anticipated his death, Dr. Stevens had the foresight to video tape his confession. Love, betrayal, and the money to back murders, you have it all ladies and gentlemen, classic motives that will lead you to find Mr. Morelli guilty of murder."

Jesus they had me. My defense had nothing. Once again the flies buzzed and the media was having a hay day jockeying for positions to best see and record the trial. The judge lifted his gavel, but never had to admonish the spectators, since they quieted down momentarily as my attorneys' looked at each other, and one stood to speak. "Mr. Morelli is notorious. Everyone in this courtroom today knows who he is. However, he is on trial for one murder, not five as the D.A. seems to be accusing him of and for that murder the DA claims to have evidence, 'incontrovertible evidence'" he added sarcastically. "All we ask today is that you keep an open mind and treat Mr. Morelli as you would anyone else brought to trial in this courtroom. If the D.A. does not bring forth the evidence promised, then it is your duty to set this man free."

And one by one the witnesses testified against me. Day in and day out a total of thirty-five witnesses' testified to my character and offered evidence to support the defense's case. Most of then told the truth, but some had been coached to lie by the prosecutors to make sure I went down. It came as little surprise that some had lied, however, I was taken back by the false testaments of Ellen and Senetti. On the stand Ellen related everything that happened that first day from the time I called her, yet one thing did not ring true. She said she noticed my rage when she mentioned that Dave and Alyssa were meeting for professional matters. My mind was confused, hadn't it been Dave that volunteered that information? He had admitted to having a meeting at noon that day, hadn't he? Why would Ellen volunteer information, especially that, and lie about it, it made no sense. Senetti lied as well, he said he knew the bat used to kill Dave had been at my house. He said he had seen it in my office when he was getting the picture of Alyssa. When I thought about it, I knew Senetti figured he was doing what he had to in order to stop me and my malevolence, even at the cost of perjuring himself. As I listened to the witnesses, regardless of the lies, I wondered if I wasn't as ruthless as they made me out to be. I knew I indeed had brutally murdered Dave and I was responsible for all the other deaths that followed in that week and worse, I would have done it over and over if I had to.

CHAPTER 22

Morelli – Final Minutes

As resigned as I am to my death, I find I am in a cold sweat. I clamp my teeth together so as not to hear them chatter I will die with dignity. No one will see my fear, nor know my thoughts. I know I am guilty of many unpardonable acts, which I deserve to die for, but the death of my wife is not one of them. My final fleeting thoughts go over it all once again for what must be the millionth time, but never so desperately as now. Who would want to frame me? Who hated me that much to make sure my final days were numbered? Who needed me out of the way? Who indeed . . . .

As the icy injection runs through my veins, I stare through the glass at those that came to see my final breaths. I was allowed to have two people of my choice. Ellen was the only one I could think of to have present and she promised to bring someone else who was important to me and she said, even more important to her. I had puzzled over that briefly, who was important to me, yet meant more to her? It didn't matter anymore. I searched the faces and found Ellen. She had her arm around the shoulders of a woman my eyes looked at and then returned to. She was the woman who had been in the courtroom. There was something, something what was it? She so reminded me of . . . . Oh my God of my lost love, yet her eyes look up at Ellen with the love I used to see in them for me. As I felt the numbness crawl up my limbs I could feel every breath getting shorter and shorter. As I fight to maintain consciousness, I search for something and yet again find my eyes on the beauty on the other side of the glass. Our eyes lock, her mouth moves. I struggle to keep my vision. She is saying "sorry". Her fingers move slowly to her cheek and I see the crossed fingers briefly touch her cheek. I know with a crystal clarity who stands on the other side of the glass, I need to tell her that it's ok, I forgive her anything, everything. A final tear runs down my face, its wetness sliding slowly to my chin. I have to show her. I can't breathe, I can't move . . . . I must. God let me . . . .let me, my fingers slowly cross as I see a tear trickle from her eyes . . . . goodbye sweetheart.

EPILOGUE

Dante

Senetti,

$\mathcal{I}$ am trying to write this letter so it can be delivered to you after my death and am having a hard time collecting my thoughts. You know it is said "dead men don't tell tales". Well, I have one for you even though I'm not going to be here to see the outcome. Lord knows I hate the thought of anyone getting one over on me, so here goes. These are my last words and better yet confessions.

I will start by saying the love I had for Alyssa was genuine and nothing she could have done would have made me cause her any harm, absolutely nothing. My rage and frustration knew no bounds. I am a man who always got what he wanted by any means necessary. I was sure I could get to the bottom of my wife's disappearance and when I found no answers, my fury was uncontrollable. I didn't think; I just acted. So, at this point I will confess my involvement in Dave's death, since I was certain he had something to do with her death. Dave was a lawyer, but as my attorney I can tell you he would do anything to win a case, I guess that's why he was my attorney for so long. It was only after his death I became completely convinced that he was telling the truth. He would never have gone through the torture I inflicted upon him if he knew anything about Alyssa. I suspect maybe he was set up as well.

So, for the record I am guilty of everything you accused me of, except I had nothing to do with the death of Alyssa. With only hours left I am experiencing an insight I never had before and if I had to guess where to start looking, I would start with Ellen. She, more than anyone, would know it would take the one person I loved above all else to be in the mix in order for me to act so irrationally. I never let anyone cross that line, but Alyssa, and Ellen knew that.

Though I am not a man who ever begs, and I have nothing to gain from this, so I am letting you know that your case is not solved. There is someone out there that knows something and is responsible. Do not let this rest or I swear to God I am the kind of bastard who will come back to haunt you. You are a good man Senetti and if life or circumstances were different, we might have been on the same side of the law. As it is, my search is ended but yours is not. I know you are the kind of man who finishes what he starts, and a lot of people have died because of this case, so don't stop looking, don't settle with my death.

Dante

Made in the USA
San Bernardino, CA
02 September 2015